Accidental Abduction

E.L. KOSLO

Table of Contents

Dedication

This book is for all the women who want a masked cinnamon roll to chase them through the woods and finger bang them against a tree.

And thank you to my laptop who held on despite getting a bit overheated during the writing of this one.

Chapter One

T HE SOUND OF GLASS shattering on the concrete floors drew my attention to the back corner of the bar. Loud voices could be heard over the music playing, and I blew out a heavy breath before placing the Pilsner glass in my hand next to the bar sink.

Fuck.

It was one of those nights. College towns were fucking chaos during the fall semester, and while my regular clientele was a little rougher around the edges, those drunken frat boys who wanted to *slum it* couldn't fucking help themselves.

Before I could hoist myself over the bar, the crowd of drunken twenty-somethings parted, and a flash of purple hair caught my attention.

My little sister's best friend had what looked to be a *frat bro*—in a pink polo shirt no less—in a headlock and was holding two fingers on his right hand in a very precarious manner. One wrong move and he'd be jerking off with his left for the foreseeable future. If she left him with anything to jerk off.

One of the bouncers followed behind her, shaking his head as she marched the jackass toward the door. Charley was fucking crazy, so if that guy touched her, he was lucky his balls were still intact and not crammed down his throat.

When she'd first asked me for a job while she was finishing grad school, I'd been hesitant, but she handled being a waitress in a crowded dive bar like a pro. She didn't let patrons get away with anything shady and brought in enough tips to keep paying her rent. Which took the pressure off me since she lived with my sister in the apartment above the bar.

"Need help?" I shouted, cupping my hand next to my mouth so Mikey could hear me.

"I think she's got it under control," he yelled back with a laugh, gesturing in front of him while Charley marched *Mr. Grabby Hands* toward the exit. Her leg shot out in front of her, kicking the door to the bar wide open as she shouted at the people loitering outside.

"Move, you fuckers. I'm trying to take out the trash."

Mikey took over from there, grabbing the guy by the back of his shirt and disappearing into the parking lot. Chances were, he'd confiscate the douche bag's keys and order him an Uber courtesy of the bar, but I was glad he was out of my establishment.

People came here to have a good time, and I wouldn't let some punk ass kids come in and start shit. Which made me sound about 90 years old, but I'd left my trouble making days behind when I'd become a business owner at 26.

If my dad's goal when he signed the bar over four years ago had been for me to take my future seriously, it'd worked.

Charley came back in, wiping her hands on her short denim skirt, smirking at me as she slipped under the overhang of the bar. She was all of five foot five, but the girl had a black belt in Taekwondo, and could put you in the hospital if you fucked with her. I'd learned years ago *not* to fuck with her.

Hazel would also give me an enormous amount of shit if I messed with her best friend. Charley was practically joined at the hip with my little sister and had been a thorn in my side since she was ten years old.

"What's up, bossman?" She reached under the bar for a shot glass, slamming it down on the counter before she grabbed a bottle of peach vodka. I watched, crossing my arms over my chest as she poured herself a shot. She winked at me before she threw it back and I tried not to let her get to me.

"What have I told you about drinking on the clock?"

She shrugged, reaching for the bottle again, but I pulled it away, blocking her with my body as she tried to get it back. "Oh, come on, I earned that."

"You earned the first one. You're done." There was no way I was sending her back out there with any more alcohol in her system. The reason she was so good at her job was because she was quick to react, so things *didn't* escalate. "Or you're back here with me the rest of the night."

She narrowed her eyes, and I was gearing up for her to give me shit, but she just huffed and glared at me. "The tips back here suck."

"Not my problem. You get drunk on my watch, I've gotta babysit you. And I don't have the time or the patience for that. If you weren't aware, you're a bit of a handful."

"Two shots won't get me drunk. You're such a buzzkill sometimes." I knew it wouldn't, but I also didn't need her stuck behind the bar with me. Every time she bartended; we'd end up slammed at the counter. I wasn't naïve enough to think it was because of my charming personality. Charley's short skirts lured them all in and I'd spend the night trying to keep up with the drooling masses competing for her attention.

My girlfriend, Vivienne, hadn't understood why I gave Hazel and Charley jobs, thinking my sister and her friend were being freeloaders. She didn't care that both of them had more than earned their places on the rotation, and business was typically higher when the two of them worked together.

It also pissed off Viv when I worked too closely with Charley. The two of them had a striking resemblance to each other, and any casual glance was construed as me being attracted to my little sister's best friend. Since I'd never thought of Charley in the same way I did about Viv, I hadn't understood why she got all bent out of shape over it, but I tried to keep my distance to keep the peace.

Hazel floated between the back of house and the bar, making sure the food service was running smoothly. While our dad had officially turned the bar over to me, he wanted her to always have a soft place to land. She was currently taking some online illustration courses, so I knew she used her tips to supplement her expenses until her illustration commissions picked up.

"Hey, sexy bartender," a high-pitched feminine voice called from the end of the bar, and I watched as Charley rolled her eyes. Before Vivienne noticed her, she spun on her heel and hoisted herself onto the bar, sliding off the far side without giving the guys at the closest table too much of a show. They kept their eyes on their drinks when they saw the glare I had aimed at them. As soon as I saw she was safely back on the floor, I returned my attention to the woman trying to get my attention.

"Can I help you, ma'am?" I asked, bracing my forearms on the worn wood. The petite platinum blonde pushed herself forward and laid a kiss on my cheek before she settled back on her stool.

"When can you get out of here?" I watched as she idly twirled a curl around her index finger. Viv was only two years younger than me at twenty-eight, but sometimes she acted—and dressed—like she was younger than my twenty-four-year-old sister. Which was fine when we'd met four years ago, but at just over thirty, I wasn't trying to relive my glory days.

Her skin-tight cropped tank top hugged her generous curves. Curves that had been what attracted me to her in the first place, and that continued to attract attention from my patrons. She had never acted on it when men hit on her, but I could tell she enjoyed the attention. Trailing my eyes down her body, I could see a sliver of the toned, artificially tanned skin of her stomach leading into a pair of tight jean shorts. It was a stark contrast to what she wore during the week, her closet full of tailored blouses and pencil skirts and sky-high heels. She may have dressed the part of the party girl on the weekends, but I knew the polished persona she cultivated at the office was who she really was.

"Bar closes in two hours. I'm the last man out tonight." Typically, I traded schedules with the other two barbacks, alternating who covered the weekends. But since I wanted to celebrate Halloween off the clock in a few days, I'd been on weekends for the last three weeks to make up for it.

"Can't you sneak out early?" she whined, cocking her head to the side. Her lashes fluttered, and she pushed out her bottom lip into a pout. A move that'd once worked on me, but I wouldn't let her manipulate me into being a shitty boss because I cared about my employee's opinions of me. "You never have time to come hang out with me anymore. You were a lot more fun when you didn't take everything with the bar so seriously."

I knew I was disappointing her, but this bar meant financial security, and I had to take it seriously if I didn't want to let everyone else down in my life. My parents were expecting me to keep the business alive, my sister depended on her income waitressing to cover the expenses for her online classes and art supplies, and my employees depended on the money they made in tips. If things started falling apart because I wanted to spend more time with my girlfriend, everyone would suffer.

"Viv, you know I can't. I'll get off at three like normal."

"But I'll be too tired to stay up by then." My temples throbbed at the shrill tone of her voice. I hated she couldn't just take no for an answer. I'd never come into her job during work hours and expect her to drop everything to keep me entertained. Just because she worked in an office during the day didn't mean *my* job during *my* work hours was any less important.

"Then maybe I'll just crash in my office." Sundays were typically when I did inventory before our weekly food delivery, so it'd be easier if I didn't have to drive back and forth. When I'd first taken over the bar, I'd lived upstairs, but when Hazel finished art school and moved back home, I'd bought a place a few blocks away, so she didn't have to live with our parents.

Viv narrowed her eyes, turning to scan the room for my sister. "You're not planning to stay in their apartment, are you?"

"No," I sighed, reaching up to re-situate my black hat on my sweaty hair. The fact that she immediately went there added to my simmering irritation. "I'll stay on the couch in my office. Down-stairs. Not upstairs."

Charley and Hazel shared the modest two-bedroom apartment above the bar now, and it was almost unrecognizable from when I lived there. My sister was girly as fuck and had painted enormous flowers on most of the walls in the living room.

I wasn't their landlord, our dad technically was, but I made sure the girls had everything they needed. And served as their handyman if anything went wrong.

"I wanted to talk to you about something." She looked upset I wasn't making myself available to her, but I had responsibilities beyond making her happy. Sometimes it felt more like I was an accessory for her to parade around than her partner. Her partner who was a grown adult with an adult job.

"After I'm done with inventory, putting away the shipment and getting next week's orders in, I'll come to your apartment."

"I guess that's fine," she sighed, but I knew she was pissed at me. I'd blown her off a lot lately. She expected me to drop everything at a moment's notice, but this bar was my future. My father hadn't kept the place running for twenty years by cutting out early and shirking his responsibilities.

Before I could dwell on how I could diffuse her attitude, the front door of the bar opened and a dozen more college students joined the melee.

"You want a drink? We're slammed, and I need to get back to work."

Viv shook her head, her face pinched in anger. But I shrugged it off and blew out a breath. When I looked back up, she was already absorbed in her phone while I escaped to the other end of the bar to serve my new patrons.

She'd been irritated with me for months after I told her I didn't want to sell my house to move into something newer together. I'd considered it, but I kept weird hours and didn't know how she'd cope with that. I also didn't want to move in together just because we'd been together for a few years.

Things had been casual between us when we started dating, and just never stopped, but she'd been hinting she wanted more lately. I just wasn't sure I could give her more.

She hadn't protested my job when we met. She'd even mistakenly thought that I was just a bartender, not the owner of the bar. My dad had still been involved in the day to day back then, and when he finally retired and I stepped into his shoes, she hadn't been happy that it meant I wasn't free whenever she called me.

As I watched her overly manicured fingers fly over her phone screen, I tried to find traces of the girl I'd fallen for. I wasn't sure she was there anymore beneath the carefully curated surface of the woman she'd become.

Chapter Two

L IFTING A CRATE OF potatoes, I carried it into the cold storage room off the kitchen and stacked it on a shelf by the door.

I stretched, rolling my shoulders before I leaned back, groaning as my back popped. Things had settled down before the last call, but I was too old to sleep on couches anymore. After spending an entire shift on my feet and then tossing and turning on the couch in my office, I was fucking tired. Plus, I desperately needed a shower because I still smelled like a bar.

"We're old as fuck," my best friend, Reid, groaned as he joined me and plunked down a crate of tomatoes. "Why can't you have one of the bartenders do this shit?"

"Because they willingly took on extra shifts this week so I could take a few days off."

"Aren't you in charge? You make the schedule, so if you want to take days off, just make them work."

"We both know it's not that easy," I laughed, stepping around him to go grab another crate from the stack by the back door. "You just gonna push one of your regulars onto another artist?"

"My situation is different. People are particular about who they want permanently inking something onto their bodies. Most people don't give a shit who's pouring their drinks." He paused, smirking at me. "Unless it's Charley. She might poison my drink."

"It's the principle of the thing. If I want them to keep working for me, I need to walk the walk. Bailing on shifts doesn't exactly foster a good working relationship or respect."

"Being a workaholic doesn't exactly foster a good romantic relationship. How's Viv dealing with you working sixty hours a week?"

Not well. I had a feeling when I headed to her apartment later, she was gonna pick a fight. Typically, fighting with her resulted in some rough, acrobatic sex, but it also didn't solve the problems between us.

But I didn't want to talk to him about this. "Like you're one to talk. How's fucking random clients working out for you?"

He glared, and I knew I'd hit the mark. "They come onto me. And it's not like I fuck them while I'm actively working on a piece. But if a hot chick gives me her number, I'm not gonna turn down a sure thing. Or a blow job in my office. Apparently, tattoos are aphrodisiacs."

"You ever considered trying to date one of them?" He'd never quite grown out of the fuckboy phase we'd both gone through in our mid 20s. It'd been fun, and no strings had been appealing at the time, but I preferred being with one person. When she wasn't pissed at me.

It allowed you time to learn what she liked, and it didn't have to be some constant struggle to perform. Stranger sex was fun for a while, but it felt kinda empty the next day. And some of those girls were wilder than I could keep up with.

Kind of like...

Nope. Not going there. I shouldn't be thinking about my sister's best friend being wild.

She never hooked up with guys from the bar, but I'd heard sounds coming from her bedroom upstairs when she didn't know I was in my office. Charley was loud, and it seemed she was into *rough* sex—especially since I could hear the banging of her headboard into the wall above me.

Part of me dreaded having to fix dents in her room when she finally moved out, because I didn't want to think about how she put them there.

It wasn't like I didn't know she was a sexual person, but thinking about it made me feel like a pervert. And knowing she took my sister out to pick up guys was something I would continue to pretend didn't happen. Hazel was a sweet girl, and she hated it when I warned guys away from her, but I didn't want to see her get taken advantage of.

"Dude, are you even listening to me?"

"What?" I shook my head, focusing on Reid and trying not to let his smirk get to me.

"I asked what your plans were for the party. What costume are you wearing?"

Viv had talked about putting together matching costumes, but I hadn't really thought about it. I was sure she'd pick something out and make me wear it. "Not sure yet. Viv said something a few weeks ago, but she hasn't shown me yet."

"You're such a fucking pussy sometimes. Why do you let her have her way all the time?"

I knew exactly why. "It's easier to do what she wants. You know how she gets."

"Do you even like her? It seems like you just stay with her cause you don't want to look for something else."

"Of course I like her. We've been together for four years."

"Then why don't you let her move in or move into her place?"

"Because I like my house and I don't want to move into one of those stupid condos she lives in." Her place looked like it belonged on an Instagram feed. I guess technically it was on hers, but it all seemed too fake. "They all look the same, and I don't fit in with all the polished professionals in that building. They'd probably think I was a vagrant or a burglar. You've seen Viv's friends."

"I know it's none of my business, but it sounds like you're making excuses. Are you staying with her because you want to be with her or because it's easier? If you ask me, I'd rather be alone than getting bossed around."

"You're right. It's not your business. And that's why you're still fucking single. You don't understand how relationships work."

He crossed his arms, and I knew he was only saying something because he was my friend, but he'd never liked Viv.

"Just because I haven't met someone that I want to spend more than a night with doesn't mean I don't understand relationships. It just means I don't waste my time on things that are bound to fail once the sex high wears off."

"And that's why you'll never be in a serious relationship. You never give anyone a chance."

"How did this suddenly become about me? I like how my life is. You're the one who is grumpy as fuck. And staying with a girl you've outgrown because it's easier than finding someone else."

"Can we just finish this so I can go home and shower before I need to go over to her place? I know you're just concerned, but you don't need to worry about me."

"Just let me know when you're ready for something different and I might let you tag along to be my wingman again. You used to be pretty good at it before Viv tried to domesticate you."

"You pick up most of your fuck friends in my bar or your shop. Not interested in bringing unnecessary drama to either of our livelihoods."

He laughed, slapping me on the back. "Fine, be a prude. Go have boring missionary sex with your vapid girlfriend before she dresses you up like a dipshit. I'm gonna make fun of your ass if she makes you wear a stupid costume."

"What are you wearing?"

He smirked, his eyebrows dancing before he leaned in. "Gonna wear my bike helmet and leather pants. Haven't decided if I'm going full shirtless or just a tight t-shirt."

"That's a costume?"

"Dude, I think you underestimate the power of a little mystery. Inked biker guy dressed up like some girl's wet dream. There's no way I'm going home alone. These college girls are into bad boys and masked men."

Sounded like he was setting himself up for trouble, but if it was all consensual, I wouldn't judge what people were into. If he wanted to have some anonymous sex wearing a motorcycle helmet and the girl was into it, that was his business. As long as he didn't do it inside my bar.

"No fucking in the back room again."

"That was one time."

"My fucking sister walked in on you balls deep in some random girl and you didn't stop. If you're gonna fuck randoms in public, take 'em next door to your shop."

"I didn't know Haz was gonna walk in. And it's not my fault she screamed and tripped over a crate of Jack in the hallway."

A few years back, I'd had to rush my sister to the emergency room when she'd walked in on him. She ended up with stitches in her leg from where she fell, and she still couldn't look Reid in the eye.

It didn't help matters when he'd kept right on fucking the girl until he came because he didn't hear Hazel's scream over the screeching of the girl he had pinned to the wall.

I'd come running to find my sister bleeding with a piece of glass from a broken whiskey bottle hanging out of her calf in the hallway and my best friend with his pants around his knees and his deflating dick hanging out.

He was lucky it hadn't been another employee, because at least I knew my sister wouldn't sue me. It wasn't the first time I'd caught people fucking in the bar—it kinda came with the territory—but I couldn't exactly kick my best friend out and ban him from the premises.

"You've just turned into this passionless version of yourself and wish you could get away with having sex in your bar," Reid teased, and I knew part of his statement was true. I had changed, but I was also determined to keep my private life away from my career.

Viv had tried to come onto me a few times when she'd stayed past closing, but promising to go down on her after I'd had a shower had distracted her enough that she finally let it go. I spent enough time in this place. I didn't want to have to sanitize the counter or the storeroom when we could just go find a bed. And fucking in a bar bathroom after drunk college kids had done God knew what all night in it had never sounded like fun.

Before I could keep arguing with him about my perfectly normal sex life, my phone buzzed in my pocket.

Viv: Are you still coming over today? We need to talk about the party.

"That her?"

"Yeah. I need to get over there. She wants to talk about the party."

"Good luck, man. Stay strong and don't cave in to some terrible couple costume. If you show up as some douchewad Disney prince, I'm taking pictures, so when you wonder where your balls went, I can show you the exact moment she snipped them off to keep in her tiny little designer purse."

He took off while I finished up, once again wondering if part of what he'd said was valid. Viv had been more of a party girl when we'd met, and we'd gotten into plenty of trouble together the first year we were hanging out, but somewhere along the way, our paths had diverged.

My degree in restaurant management had made it a seamless transition when my dad decided spending eight to ten hours a day standing behind a bar wasn't what he wanted anymore. I couldn't blame him. He'd given a lot of himself to the bar and when my mom had cut back on her hours at the hospital, he'd wanted to rekindle some parts of their relationship they'd lost along the way.

They were disgustingly in love again after settling into partial retirement. They finally had a good work-life balance and could focus on their relationship. I knew his hours had caused problems between them when we were younger. Haz didn't remember the hushed conversations behind closed doors, or the months he'd slept in the apartment above the bar when I was in high school.

Part of me recognized the signs of a crumbling relationship when Viv harped on me for working too much, but I never gave her shit when she'd travel for work once a month.

Another text came through as I was locking up, and I knew I'd stalled long enough.

> *Viv: If you're not coming over here, at least have the decency to let me know.*

> *Hudson: Showering and then I'll be over. Give me 45 minutes.*

My bike was tucked under an overhang next to the back door in a small fenced in area secured with a padlock because some drunken idiot had tried to ride off with it a few years ago.

The weather would start changing soon, but as long as I could, I'd take my bike to work. There was something invigorating about taking sharp turns at speed and feeling my stomach bottom out as I wove through the winding mountain roads. Viv hated riding with me, so if I knew we had plans, I'd take my restored Chevelle to work, but even lately she'd be badgering me to sell it to buy a more *sensible* car.

She drove a Tesla, and while it was nice, there was no way I'd be caught dead in a car that pretentious. Classic muscle cars had always been my passion, and with all the hours I'd put into restoring mine, I wasn't willing to give it up.

Twenty minutes later, I stowed my bike in the garage and traded it out for my car after a quick shower. I took the short drive into town to Viv's condo where she met me at the door. Her hair was thrown up into a carefully sculpted messy bun and she had on a pair of designer sweats. This was about as casual as she'd get, and for once I wished she'd just relax and be herself. Twenty-four-year-old Viv hadn't been afraid to wander around her place with her hair down in chaotic blonde waves and one of my old shirts. I hadn't seen that Viv in a long time.

When I looked at her now, I often wondered if I'd hallucinated the girl I'd met.

"Finally," she sighed, pulling the door open wider and gesturing me into her pristine looking place. "We need to talk, Hudson."

Chapter Three

"**S**ORRY I KEPT YOU waiting for so long. Shipment was bigger this week with the party, and it took a little longer to get everything put away than I'd expected," I apologized, leaning down to kiss her cheek. She scoffed and leaned away, my lips brushing the air as I walked past her. She slammed the front door harder than seemed necessary and followed me into the living room.

"Wouldn't have had to wait if you'd come over here last night like I'd asked you to."

Shit. Seemed like Viv was in a mood. Not that it absolved me of what she'd said. I had been prioritizing the bar over her for months. Typically, I'd push back and remind her I had tasks I couldn't drop whenever she wanted me to.

"You wanted to talk about the party?" Changing the subject and avoiding a fight seemed like a better option.

She crossed the apartment, roughly pulling a garment bag from the coat closet. "I picked the costumes up yesterday."

She flung it over the back of the couch, and I watched as she unzipped the bag, wincing when I saw the purple leather jacket inside.

"What?" she huffed, pulling the hangers out and draping them across the back of the couch. "Do you have a problem with what I picked out? You're obsessed with that comic book girl. I thought you'd like this one. And we both know how good I look in tiny shorts and fishnets."

"I'm not going shirtless." She clearly picked out the Jared Leto era 'Joker' costume, but I'd rather wear a purple suit over being shirtless in an ugly purple crocodile skin jacket.

Part of me was stoked she'd be dressed up like a scantily clad comic book villainess, but I wasn't sold on the couples costumes.

"You're so vanilla sometimes. What's the point of having all the ink if you're going to cover it up?"

"I own the bar, Viv. Coming in shirtless, covered in face paint, and wearing a tacky purple trench coat isn't my idea of fun."

"Nothing is your idea of fun lately. You used to be more exciting. We used to have fun together."

"We still have fun." When I had weekends off, she dragged me all over the place to things I had no interest in. Unless it came to my hours at the bar, I let her do whatever she wanted when we were together. I just enjoyed spending time with her. At least I used to. "I worked a shit ton of extra hours lately so we could go to the party instead of me working it. I don't know what else you want from me."

"I want you to be spontaneous again. You used to be edgy and adventurous. Now you just obsess over the bar and hang out with Reid playing video games when I'm busy. When was the last time you did something that gave you a rush?"

"We... I..." Stunned, I sat down on her couch, resting my elbows on my knees as I tried to absorb her words. Maybe I had gotten too used to my routine to deviate from it. "What kind of spontaneous things do you have in mind?"

"It's not spontaneous if I have to tell you something. God, I wished you'd just figure it out by now. I'm so tired of my girlfriends bragging about their sex lives and me being like *'yeah, Hudson came over after his shift and fucked me missionary in my bed before he passed out.'* Do you want to know some of the stories I hear from them? I feel like I settled for a dud that looked like a bad boy."

"Viv, what the fuck? That was a cheap shot. You know I can't..."

"Yeah, that's the problem. All I hear is '*I can't.*' You *could* if you gave a shit." She crossed her arms over her chest, staring daggers at me across the space that divided us.

"What do you want?" Her girlfriends looked like little clones of each other, so I wasn't sure what kind of dirty shenanigans they were getting up to. They seemed like the type to be afraid of breaking a nail rather than engaging in adventurous sex.

"Beth and Travis went camping last month, and he fucked her up against a tree. She had bark burn for a week. You don't even want to leave the bedroom, Hudson. I feel like I'm never gonna get what they have. Marcy said Mason chased her through the woods behind their house with a mask, then carried her back to his car and they fucked in the driveway. When the fuck am I gonna get something like that?"

Having met those people, that was a bit of a surprise, but maybe she was right. We were still young, and we didn't have any kids. Maybe we needed to spice things up a bit. Something needed to change because it seemed neither of us were happy. "Where did your friends even come up with that stuff?"

"If you were around more, you'd know we have a spicy book club. They've all convinced their guys to try out scenes from the books, but you won't even let me fuck you in your office."

"You were trying to get me to leave the bar unmanned on a Saturday during a rush. Do you have any idea what kind of chaos would happen if I left during that?" It was bad enough that she guilt tripped me because of my work hours, but when she tried to manipulate me into sex when I was on shift, I'd been pissed.

"Get someone else to watch the bar for once. God, Hudson, I want to feel like I'm more than some toy you just play with when you have time."

"What do you want me to do? What's something you want to try from one of your books?" If it wasn't too off the wall, I'd try it out. Maybe we needed to find the spark again. I hadn't realized she was so unhappy with how things were between us.

"You know those white ghost masks from those movies that came out in the late 90s?" I knew what she was talking about. We'd watched the first movie together once, but she hadn't really seemed into it. "I wouldn't be opposed to you chasing me or pretending to kidnap me wearing one of those."

The words Reid had uttered about girls being into masked men came to mind, and I started planning in my head. "When?"

"That's exactly what the problem is." She crossed her arms over her chest, tapping her foot as she glared at me. "I'm not going to tell you when you need to be spontaneous. That defeats the entire purpose. You should just do it."

"How am I supposed to know when a good time is to plan something like this? Am I just going to show up one day and tell you to run? What else do I wear? Do I tie you up and take you into the woods or something?" Gripping my hair, I roughly ran my fingers through the damp strands, trying not to let this overwhelm me. What she was asking for theoretically sounded reasonable, but what happened if it didn't go as planned? She'd just use this as another thing to be upset about.

Viv looked defeated as she sat next to me on the couch, pulling her leg beneath her and placing her hand on my shoulder. "I've loved you for a long time, Hudson. But maybe it's time we acknowledged we want different things. Things I don't think you can give me."

"What the hell is that supposed to mean?"

"Maybe we should go to the party separately, try hanging out with other people. See if someone else might be a better fit."

What the fuck? "It sounds like you're breaking up with me *and* you want to come pick guys up at my bar during a party that I planned because you wanted one."

"Is that such a bad idea? We both aren't happy."

"Since when am I not happy? Don't throw this shit on me. I bend over backward to make time for you when my schedule allows it." But sometimes I had to change plans because I was needed at the bar. And she was pissed when it happened and regularly gave me the silent treatment. But I always tried to make it up to her. Clearly that wasn't enough.

"I'll return your costume to the shop. If you aren't excited at the idea of doing something that would make me happy, we clearly need to hit the pause button. I want to stay friends. I still care about you, but I just need to see if something different fulfills what I want in a partner. We're getting older and I don't want to waste time on something that will fall apart if you don't put in more effort."

"So, this is it? You're breaking up with me because I don't initiate spontaneous sex with you?" While it'd been the initial draw in our relationship, it seemed insane for her to break up with me because she thought our sex life had gotten stale. We'd both invested four years into being a couple. She wasn't just some fuck toy to me.

"There are other things, too. Can you honestly tell me we're looking for the same future together?" she asked, sounding exasperated.

She was acting like I didn't do anything for our relationship. Like every nice thing I planned for her on my days off, or going on outings with her vapid friends and their equally douchey boyfriends wasn't doing what she wanted. But of course, I was the one being unreasonable.

"This isn't working out for me in more than just one area. Maybe we need to take some time. I don't want to force you to want me. If things don't work out, we can check in with each other in a few months and see if this is worth rekindling."

It seemed like she was talking in circles. She wanted me to be more spontaneous, but only because I wanted to, and then she wanted to keep me on the hook if things didn't go how she wanted with dating other guys.

"Maybe you're right. I'm gonna head out. Guess I'll...see you later."

Her eyes flashed with something that looked an awful lot like panic, but if she didn't want me here, I'd leave. Before she roped me back in because whenever we fought like this, the problem was always me. I'd clearly let her down according to her, over some-thing that in the scheme of things seemed pretty damn superficial.

She took a breath and masked her expression. "Don't be mad, baby. I'm doing this for us."

Viv inched forward, kissing just below the corner of my mouth. Where I'd once felt a spark when she touched me, felt flat. In the past, I would have turned and kissed her back, but I needed to get out of here and clear my head. She tried to hug me as I left, but my arms hung limply at my sides.

"This isn't goodbye. This is just us evaluating what we really want in life and deciding if what we have is worth coming back to. You know this is what's best for us, don't you, baby?" she asked, stroking the skin on my cheek and lifting an eyebrow. I'd seen this look many times when she was trying to get someone to do something they didn't want to. "I'll come find you at the party if you'll save a dance for me."

Looked like I had a shitload of soul searching to do before this party. I could either try to prove her wrong, and plan something to win her back, or I could get really drunk and pass out in my office after spending all night as Reid's wingman.

Either way, I was fucked.

Chapter Four

Hudson

"**I** DON'T WANT TO say I told you so, but I fucking told you, dude."

Glaring at my best friend as I wiped down the glasses lined up on the bar, I regretted confiding in him about what had gone down with Viv at her place. "Shut the fuck up, asshole."

"Hey, you're the one who confided in me. I didn't ask to get pulled into your relationship drama."

"Didn't stop you from giving your opinion."

"And what did I fucking tell you? I told you not to settle for some spoiled brat who doesn't appreciate you."

His words stung, but a part of me felt like the future I envisioned was falling right out from under me.

"Shit. Man, I don't like that look on your face. What are you doing?" Reid had known me for almost twenty years, so he knew when I set my mind to accomplishing something.

Taking a breath, I decided I was not letting the last four years go down the drain without a fight. "What I should have done a while ago."

"Dump her and run?" He laughed. I knew he was trying to find humor in the situation, but I was panicking here.

"No, you ass. I'm going to be the guy she started dating again." There had to be a way for me to keep her interested. I knew I'd let the bar take over my life, but I hadn't realized it was this bad. Maybe her trying to break things off was the wake-up call I needed. I was thirty, not dead, so I needed to live my life outside the four walls I'd sequestered myself in since taking over.

"Fuck," he sighed, giving me the look everyone seemed to give me lately—disappointment. "Don't do that, man. They always say they want the bad boy, but no woman over twenty-four really wants to end up with the bad boy. They want to fuck the bad boy until the endorphins wear off."

"Is that why you—"

"Don't bring me into this again. Viv fucked you until you had to grow up. She wanted the motorcycle and the tattoos—you're welcome, by the way." He smirked as he surveyed the sleeves on both my arms. He'd spent countless hours designing and inking the elaborate patterns onto my skin. I rolled my eyes, but his smile just widened. "She didn't want the nice guy with the big heart and the big dic—"

"Okay, I get it. But I have to try, or I'll always regret it." Letting our relationship end like this didn't feel right. Viv walking out of my life right now felt like a punch to the gut. "Maybe I have become this complacent guy who only focuses on the bar. We were in love, and now I don't recognize either of us."

"And what if you regret it because you do whatever it is that you think you need to do?"

Only one way to find out.

REID LEFT ME TO wallow in my office, contemplating where I went from here. There were only two options:

Cut my losses and focus on the things in my life I could control so I could enter my next relationship in a healthier place.

Re-evaluate what I wanted and prioritize Viv the way she wanted me to so we could repair things and move on from here.

Both options sounded daunting, but either way, I wanted a partner to share my life with. Someone who understood me and was willing to make compromises and support each other. That meant I needed to be a supportive partner, too.

The itch to get on my bike and just ride sounded appealing, but I had a mountain of paperwork to do and details to complete so we were ready for the party in a few days.

My phone vibrating next to my laptop interrupted my chaotic thoughts, and I sighed as I saw *Mom* scrolling across the screen.

"Hey." My voice sounded strained, and I knew she'd pick up on it, but I was too tired to care.

"Do I need to send your dad down there?" she asked, immediately going into problem-solving mode. "I told him you might need help getting everything ready for this party. That's why he never bothered to do anything more than put up a few decorations for holidays. It wasn't a party type of establishment. But I guess since those college kids seem to like the atmosphere in there, you've gotta cater to the new demographics."

If I let her, she'd just keep talking, filling in both sides of the conversation herself.

"I think Haz and I have got it handled, mom. But I appreciate that you guys are willing to step in if we need you. You're welcome to stop by and see the place before the party if you want to double check that we did it right. But I promise we've got it under control."

She laughed, knowing that I was teasing her about her perfectionist nature. She liked to have things done a certain way, but she also knew when to let Hazel and me forge our own paths.

"Your dad and I will be here passing out candy, but I know you two will make it fun. You'll both have to come over next week and tell us all about it before we leave for our trip. We can have a family dinner. Just let me know what works for you and Viv, and I'll call Hazel. Maybe we can invite Charley and Reid too. Make a dinner party of the whole thing."

Biting my lip, I contemplated not telling her about Viv. I could stick to my usual excuses and just let her focus her energy on Hazel and Charley.

"How is your sweet girlfriend? Is she excited you're taking her to the party instead of working?"

Not sure I would describe her as sweet, but Viv put on a good show in front of my parents. They thought rainbows shot out of her ass. The way I used to. Now I wasn't so sure what I thought.

"I think she's looking forward to the party," I sighed, closing my eyes. "But she's not going with me."

The line was silent for a moment, but my mother wasn't a naïve person. She knew how to read between the lines.

"Did you break up with that poor girl? I told you that you needed to learn from your father's mistakes. That bar will still be there at the end of the day, but it can't talk to you or make you feel loved."

Hearing the concern in her voice just confirmed that maybe I *was* the cause of all of this. I'd made selfish decisions and my relationship had suffered.

"She isn't getting what she needs from me anymore." Wasn't that what she'd told me?

"Oh, Hudson." I hated that she sounded disappointed in me. "Do I need to have the same conversation with you that I had with your father?"

"Probably," I mumbled. They were still together after thirty-five years, so clearly, they'd done something right.

"You need to figure out what you want out of life beyond the four walls of that building. There was a reason that Grandpa was divorced, and Grandma lived on the other side of the country. Owning a bar can be stressful, and if you let it, it'll take over your life."

Clearly, it already had.

"But if you have a partner there that keeps you grounded, someone who pulls you back when you get too deep, then you can live the life you want. You've done a good job of getting the business where it needed to be when your dad retired. He was tired. And while I know he used me as an excuse, he wanted to travel more and spend time out in the garage building things."

"I knew about the separation," I confessed, remembering how hard things were between them before I left for college.

"You didn't know everything, Hudson. Your dad was the one who moved out. He was afraid that his lifestyle wasn't fair to me because with my schedule opposite of his, we never saw each other. He told me he wanted to sell the bar, and I tried to talk him out of it, knowing he loved that place and wanted to pass it down to you."

I'd always thought it was the other way around.

"And how did you change things? I thought you two were going to get divorced."

"A grand gesture," she said simply, a smile in her voice. "I showed up at the bar one night, joined him behind the bar and told him I was going to move to a different shift. If our schedules conflicting was what he was worried about, I solved the problem. You two were old enough to get yourselves off to school and didn't need me around after, so I started working night shifts a few days a week so we could both be home during the day."

"I don't know..." I wasn't sure that solution would work for Viv and me, but maybe I could hire another bartender and do more of my work during the day while she was at work. If I made more of an effort to let others step in and help at the bar instead of doing everything myself, maybe that'd relieve some of the stress.

"Just think about it. Start small. Maybe making a small gesture will help things along."

"Maybe..." At this point, it wouldn't hurt for me to make a few changes and see where things went.

"I've got faith in you, and you need to have some in yourself too. Just jump, and if you two are meant to work things out, she'll catch you. Everything will work out how it's meant to."

Chapter Five

Hudson

V IV HAD SAID SHE wanted a grand gesture. She said she wanted someone exciting and adventurous who'd help bring her fantasies to life. A few years ago, I *was* her fantasy. I could do this. I *would* do this.

Even if I wasn't sure if I could do this.

"Fuck, Huds. Stop. You're making *me* nervous. Everything will be fine. I promise we have all the details for the party in place. People will have fun. *You* will enjoy yourself for once. I told you we had this all under control. Charley will be on for the first two hours before Gianna takes over for her, and I can stay longer if they need me. But we don't need *you*."

Blowing out a breath, I braced my palms on the edge of the bar, gripping the surface until my knuckles turned white. I knew Hazel was just trying to reassure me, but she didn't know why I was currently freaking out. If she did, she'd probably be telling me I was a dumbass, like Reid had.

Hazel and my girlfriend—or whatever she was now—had never gotten along, despite being slightly closer in age. I wasn't sure if it was Viv's loud distaste for her best friend, or if Hazel just genuinely didn't like her. Viv had tried so hard when we started dating to include Hazel in things, even trying to set her up on blind dates with some of her friends, but their relationship had never blossomed beyond having me in common.

"You've taken nights off before," Hazel said quietly, placing her hand in between my shoulder blades and rubbing until the tension drained away. She was right. I had taken nights off before and things at the bar had been fine. I had a team that knew how to manage a crowd and just because there was a party didn't mean they couldn't handle it.

"I know. I know you guys have got this. I trust you, but tonight is different. If things go off the rails, I don't know if I can fix this."

Hazel leaned against the side of the bar, leaning over until I looked at her face. "Is the bar in trouble or something? You would've told me if something was wrong, right? I know you're the one in charge, but Dad wanted us to be partners."

"Yeah," I sighed, dropping my head forward. "The bar is fine. I've just got other things on my mind right now." Like trying to find my balls to pull off my plans for later. They'd been stashed in Viv's purse for so long. I wasn't sure if I still knew how to use them.

"Are things okay with you?" she asked, and I sighed loudly, closing my eyes. "You're not sick or something, are you? I know you've been stressed lately, but if something else is going on, we can get coverage for you behind the bar."

Fuck. Now my little sister was convinced I was dying.

No, Haz, I'm just being a dramatic little bitch because my girlfriend sort of dumped me, and I have one shot to get her to take me seriously. And if I fuck that up, I'm not sure what I'm going to do.

"I'm fine."

"Is..." she hesitated, her hand squeezing my shoulder. "Is something going on with you and Viv? She's normally up your ass when you're here for holidays, and I haven't seen her today. Actually, I haven't seen her for a few days. She is coming, right?"

I have no fucking clue.

She'd given me the impression that she was going to come tonight, despite things being strained between us. But she hadn't texted me since I left her apartment, and I was too afraid to text her before I'd decided to go through with this.

"I don't know. Things are..." I wasn't even sure how to explain what was going on in my head to her. "...complicated. She'll be here, but I'm not sure if she's coming for me."

"Did you guys break up?"

Yes. No. I had no fucking clue.

"Kinda. I guess. Things are just a little strained right now. But I've got a plan to show her that I can change and be what she wants."

Hazel pushed on my shoulder, gripping my jaw and turning my face toward her. My sister was a tiny thing, but she had a fire underneath the shy demeanor. "What did she do?"

"She didn't do..."

She pushed my shoulder, and I watched the concern on her face morph into something a little bit unhinged. Charley may scare me, but a pissed off Hazel was kinda terrifying. "Is she trying to get you to sell the bar again? I told her it'd never happen and..."

"Wait, what?" I stopped her growly rant with a hand on her shoulder. "When did she say anything about selling the bar?"

"A few months ago, I overheard her and one of her little minions talking about you two buying a house together once you'd sold the bar. Charley lit into her for trying to manipulate you into selling, but I told her the bar was never going to be for sale. She tried to walk it back by telling me I'd mistaken what she'd said, but I heard everything Viv told her friend. She was so absorbed in their conversation she hadn't realized I'd been standing there the whole time."

This was the first time I'd heard about it, but maybe Hazel had just misinterpreted what she'd heard. We had been talking about getting a house together, but we couldn't agree on what we wanted and neither of us had been willing to compromise at the time.

"I'm not selling, so please don't worry about that." This place was as much my dream as it had been to my father and his father before him.

"I know. You would've talked to me first. And I know you'd never do that to Dad."

It'd been a point of contention when I'd graduated high school that he wanted to make sure I actually wanted the bar, not only because I felt obligated. Once I'd gotten my degree in restaurant management a few years later, he'd retired within a year, knowing his legacy was safe.

"But quit changing the subject. What's going on? Do I need to let the door know not to let her in? If she hurt you, I'll make sure she never steps foot in this place again."

Chuckling, I stepped back and grabbed a bar rag, distracting myself by wiping up nonexistent water spots on the taps. "No, actually, I need you to have the door let me know when she gets here. I'm working on a surprise for her, and I need some time to get things prepared."

She turned her head, scrunching up her nose. "You're not proposing to her, are you?"

A resounding, *Fuck, no,* was almost out of my mouth before I stopped myself from saying it out loud. Why? I wasn't sure. But I didn't have time to dwell on why the hell that was my gut reaction. Just because I wasn't ready to ask her to marry me now didn't mean I wouldn't be ready once things were repaired between us. But I needed to pull this off first.

"Not today," I replied absently. Hazel's eyes narrowed, but the back door opening halted whatever she was going to say. Her eyes widened, and for a moment I worried that Viv had shown up early and it'd ruin what I had planned. But Reid's voice had my sister scurrying out the other side of the bar before I could even turn around.

"You ready for tonight, fuck face? It's going to be epic."

When I turned around, I saw what had my sister fleeing. "Fuck, put on a damn shirt, you asshole."

"What? Why?" he asked, placing his motorcycle helmet on the edge of the bar. "I'm already in my costume."

"We serve food here. No one wants to see your nipples while they're eating. Cover that shit up." Reid was wearing a pair of leather pants with a chrome studded belt, his black combat boots...and that was about it. I knew he'd warned me, but I hadn't thought he'd start the night out showing off his pierced nipples. I figured he'd take off his shirt once he was drunk, but I'd be gone by then, so it wouldn't be my problem.

"I told you what I was wearing. Charley didn't seem to have a problem with it when I passed her in the back. Why are you being such a prude?"

"Didn't you see how disgusted Hazel was? She practically ran away as soon as she saw you."

"If you hadn't noticed, your sister runs away every time she sees me, so it's not just when my nipples are out." He thought he was being charming, but I was the one who'd had to pay for her therapy—both physical and psychological—after her accident caused by his inability to keep his dick in his pants.

"Well, maybe if you hadn't scarred her for life with your fuck boy antics, then my sister wouldn't hate my best friend."

"Did you really just call me a fuck boy? What are we, eighteen-year-old girls? I thought you'd be the last person to slut shame me, but sorry for having an active sex life you're clearly jealous of. Get your head out of your ass, dude. This is the chance for you to find yourself again. Don't waste it."

Was that what I was doing? Had I been trying too hard to cling to a woman who didn't want me instead of finding what I really wanted out of life?

"Did you see what Charley had on?" he asked, lowering his voice as he joined me behind the bar.

"Are you seriously going to be that much of a pervert? She's Hazel's best friend. They're not even..."

"She's twenty-five, Hudson. Charley's not a little girl anymore. Neither is Hazel, for that matter." My eyes widened when I noticed his gaze focused on my little sister across the room.

"Are you fucking kidding me? Stop staring at my baby sister like that." His eyes lingered on Hazel and Charley standing by the door to the kitchen. I still couldn't make out what Charley had on because my sister was blocking my view of what her best friend was wearing.

"Like what? I was just looking across the room," he said, smirking at me. He knew how protective I was of Hazel. And I didn't like the way his face softened while he gazed at her.

"Don't even fucking think about it. She's too young for you."

"Six years is hardly an age gap," he laughed, and then held up his palms in supplication when I glared in his direction. "I'm just saying. How is the four years between you and Viv any different than the six between Hazel and I?"

"Let's get this fucking straight, there is no Hazel and you. And I didn't know Viv when she was in middle school. Charley is just like a..." While she was gorgeous and I wished I had half of her self-confidence, I'd never let myself think about Charley as anything other than Hazel's best friend.

"I know you're not this blind. Charley is a fucking smoke show, and you know it. I've seen you watching her from behind the bar. You're attracted to her."

Was I? I know sometimes I found myself watching her across the crowded bar, but I was just making sure she had the floor handled. She was a force to be reckoned with, but she was still smaller than half the men who hung out in the bar. Watching them hit on her made my protective instincts flare.

"Attraction doesn't have to be acted on. Despite your track record," I teased, but he just rolled his eyes.

"You know I'm right. Open your eyes, man. There are plenty of women who'd love to take Viv's place and won't treat you like an accessory."

"What does that mean? Charley isn't interested in me. So why are we even talking about her?"

He leaned against the bar, blocking my line of sight to the two girls...women, on the other side of the room. "Keep your eyes open to new possibilities. I know Viv was comfortable, and you thought you loved her. But if she's pushing you away because she's not getting what she needs from the relationship, maybe you need to let go."

"I do love her," I responded weakly, continuing to stare over his shoulder at the blonde standing next to my sister.

Didn't I?

"WHY DON'T YOU GO change?" Hazel took the black roll of crepe paper from my hands. I'd been hanging streamers in all the doorways for decoration. Charley and Hazel had been busy decorating the tables and walls. I'd been trying to focus on the plan in my head and not watching them. "Unless you're wearing that."

"What's wrong with this?" I asked, looking down at the black, long-sleeved shirt with a glow in the dark skull I'd thrown on this afternoon before heading to the bar. It was what I'd worn every Halloween for the last few years.

"It's a costume party. You did get a costume, right?"

There was a backpack sitting on my desk with the costume I'd planned on throwing on before the party started. While part of me thought it'd be a good idea to dress up as the comic book villain Viv had wanted me to be, I'd changed my mind when I'd stopped by the costume shop close to campus. Thankfully, they had what I needed to pull off my plan for tonight.

Knowing Hazel wouldn't approve of my plans to win my ex back, I just shrugged. "I was thinking maybe I'd cover the bar if we get busy later. I don't need a costume to pour drinks."

"Don't even fucking think about it. You've been pulling extra shifts to have tonight off. Enjoy yourself. Charley and I are on for the initial rush, and then we'll change into our costumes later. You've gotta step out from behind that bar sometimes."

"I can pitch in on both expo and the bar if you guys just want to change now and take the night off. We've handled busy nights with less staff before."

My sister forcibly grabbed me by the shoulders and pushed me toward the back office, growling. "I love you but get a fucking life."

I wanted to scold my sister for cursing, like I had been for a decade, but maybe she was right.

REID HAD GONE BACK to his shop for a bit before he needed to be back for the party, so I snuck into the office, pulling out the payroll paperwork I needed to have done for next week. If tonight went how I hoped it would, I'd be busy for the next few days.

"Hey, Hud," a voice sang from the doorway, and I looked up, fighting the urge to stare at the outfit Charley was supposedly wearing. Her tiny skintight denim shorts showed off her toned thighs, and the tank top she wore barely contained the push-up bra visible above the neckline.

"Stop calling me Hud," I grunted, returning my attention to the files on my computer. Reid's comments had to be getting to me, because I couldn't be getting turned on by my sister's best friend showing a bit of cleavage, but I was. I *so* was.

"Want me to call you *son* instead? Into a little mommy play there, big guy?" she teased, leaning over the back of the chair across from my desk. My fingers twitched on the keys of my laptop as I got an even better view down her top. If she shifted forward slightly, I could just barely make out the outline of her nip—

No, idiot. Quit being a pervert.

"I hate you," I growled, refusing to look at her.

"No, you don't. You fucking adore me." She was right, I did, but those once platonic feelings were getting blurred.

"Stop cursing, Char."

"I just turned twenty-five, Hud. I can say the word fucking. Here, I'll tell you a secret," she said, stepping around the chair and bracing her hands flat on my desk as she leaned in and lowered her voice to a whisper. "I can do it too."

Do not think about her fucking. Or naked. Or how I'd like to push the papers off my desk and lay her across it to peel those tiny shorts off and bury by face in...

"Don't you have a job to do?" She really needed to leave me alone because I couldn't afford to have any distractions. It had to be the nerves making me have these inappropriate thoughts about the wrong woman. Winning Viv back was my goal right now, not fantasizing about my sister's friend.

"Yes." She still hadn't moved—her cleavage eye level—but I refused to look anywhere but at the screen.

"So go do it." *Please go away.*

"Yes Sir, boss man." Her teasing tone had me looking up, just in time to see her sassy salute, her breasts jiggling as she moved her arm.

"My name is Hudson." And I was a dumbass.

"Yeah, I know. See you later, handsome."

My body sighed in relief as she walked out my office door, her hips swaying as she left. Leaning forward to brace my elbows on the desk, I buried my face in my hands, going over the plan in my head again. Tonight had to work.

Chapter Six

"ONLY TWENTY MINUTES LEFT," Hazel sighed, leaning against the wall next to the expo window of the kitchen where I'd been trying to catch my breath. Things had been nuts since we opened, the bouncers having to turn people away once we hit capacity.

"It's hot as fuck in here," I groaned, pushing the stray hairs from my ponytail behind my ears. Thank God for dry shampoo, because I'd definitely need a touch-up after I changed my costume. Not that it was much different from what I had on. Throw on a T-shirt, put my hair up into pigtails and spray the newly stripped ends turquoise, pull on my knee-high boots, put on my mask and I'd be ready.

As crazy as it was tonight, I needed to let off some steam, and I needed to quit obsessing over Hudson. He'd been moody the last few days, ever since Vivienne cut things off between the two of them. Reid said they were on a break or something, but that rarely meant people were getting back together.

Hudson had been tightlipped about the whole thing. The only reason I knew was because his best friend was terrible at keeping secrets. And I totally understood how Hudson felt. He had a right to be upset over the idea of a four-year relationship ending. But he deserved so much better.

Not that it meant I'd go after him or anything, but the old feelings I'd pushed down once things got serious with her were bubbling back to the surface. Even when he was grumpy and couldn't take a joke, I still wanted to be around him. I just wished he saw me as something other than Hazel's best friend.

"Order up!" the cook yelled through the window. Hazel and I made eye contact, both spinning to grab the plates of greasy bar food from the counter. Only twenty more minutes and I could find some cute younger guy to take upstairs and fuck away any thoughts of Hudson. It was second nature by now, my coping mechanism for dealing with messy feelings that I shouldn't be having. Hudson was the ultimate forbidden fruit, and I was dying to take a bite.

BY THE TIME I made it back to the apartment to change—over an hour later than I'd hoped—I was half tempted to face plant into my mattress and say fuck the whole party. I still had a paper to finish writing, and if I was hungover tomorrow, I'd have zero motivation to finish it on my day off.

The only reason I even wanted to go was because it'd been weeks since I let myself properly blow off steam. Or blow anything, for that matter. And I had a feeling the toys in my bedside drawer wouldn't take the edge off much longer.

Pulling off my sweaty clothing, I headed for the bathroom. A whore's bath was in order. I smelled like greasy fried food, and while I was sure some guys were into that, I was not. After soaping up my tits, slit, and armpits, I laid my forehead on the cool tiles and tried to relax.

Balancing my grad school hospitality and tourism classes along with my job at the bar had been nuts lately, and I was ready to be done. Luckily, I only had next semester to finish up. Once I had that degree in hand, transitioning to a big girl job would be infinitely easier, but the thought of what came next still gave me more anxiety than it should.

I continuously tried to convince myself it was because Hazel needed me, and I would have separation anxiety from my best friend. But walking away from the girlish crush I'd had on Hudson for over a decade—now that he was almost single again—was going to be a challenge all on its own. My sole focus should be on my job with my aunt and uncle after graduation in the next town over, even if it took me away from Sage Springs. Not fantasizing about riding the dick I'd been picturing in my head since I hit puberty.

Leaving home behind wasn't something I wanted to do, but I also didn't want to play crowd control with unruly college guys for the rest of my life. Hudson hadn't hesitated to give me a job so I could keep up with my living expenses. Then he'd offered to let Hazel and I live above the bar and charged us barely anything for rent. I knew the bar was his life, but I was ready for something different.

"Are you ready to go yet?" Hazel yelled from the hallway, and I blew out a heavy breath before rinsing off.

Turning off the shower, I yelled back my response, pretending I was excited about going to the party and not secretly dreading having to pretend I was as much fun as everyone else thought I was. "Five minutes, bitch, and then it's on."

Pulling open my dresser, I cursed as I realized that I didn't have any clean underwear. My laundry basket had been overflowing for over a week because I didn't have time to take it to the laundromat across town. And there was no way in hell I was going to Hudson's house to do it like Hazel did.

"What's taking so long?" Hazel asked, appearing in my doorway dressed in her angel costume. She was just adorable enough to pull it off with her brownish red hair and big blue eyes. But she definitely didn't look angelic with the skirt showing off most of her thighs.

Hudson was going to kill me if he thought I had anything to do with her costume, but she'd picked this one out all on her own. I was so proud. My once shy, wallflower best friend was finally embracing her sensuality with open arms. And if the glint in her eyes was any indication, she wanted to with open legs as well.

"All I have clean are these." Pinching a pair of the oversized boy shorts I wore during my period between my fingers and cringed.

"Ew. Do you want a pair of mine?" While I appreciated the offer, I had a bit more junk in my trunk than my petite best friend, so I'd just be trading oversized underwear for undersized ones, and not in the cute, slutty way. It'd be in the cut off my circulation and leave behind bruises way. I liked to earn my markings in a much kinkier way.

"Nah, I'll make it work." Eyeing where I'd tossed my cut off denim shorts on the bed, I gauged if they were tight enough that there wouldn't be a risk of indecent exposure on the dance floor downstairs.

"You're such a slut," she laughed as I pulled on the shorts, going commando, making sure that there wasn't any chance they'd show off something that'd get me in trouble.

"It's not like I'm going downstairs in my underwear like some people," I teased, giving the almost see through lace bodysuit Hazel was wearing underneath her tiny skirt a pointed look.

"We'll just have to avoid Hudson. He'll lose his shit if he sees me like this."

Hudson had always been overprotective of Hazel, especially since she'd always been too trusting for her own good. In high school and college, I'd been the reckless one while she was the well-behaved good girl. I'd tried to get her out of her shell in the last year or so, but he'd continued treating her like she was a sixteen-year-old virgin. And while she'd never confirmed it because she didn't like to kiss and tell, I suspected her V card had yet to be punched.

"He can suck it. You look hot, and I can guarantee you still have more covered up than some of the girls downstairs." We'd seen several already tonight who were spilling out of their tight costumes.

"Did you see the one Reid was dancing with before you came up here?"

"Can't say that I was keeping track of him, but I'm sure you were."

She blushed and tucked a loose curl behind her ear before she looked away. Hazel had been crushing on Reid for years, but she'd avoided him since the incident where she walked in on him fucking some girl in the stock room downstairs. But that didn't mean she hadn't continued to watch him from afar. Her crush was blatantly more obvious than mine on her brother. To everyone *but* Reid.

"Once we put on our masks, they won't be able to tell who we are."

That's what I was counting on. Tonight, I wanted anonymity. I didn't want to be Hazel's best friend, and more importantly, I didn't want to be Charley, the ball-busting waitress. My reputation for booting handsy guys from the bar had exactly the opposite effect I wanted it to tonight. I wanted to find someone to put his hands all over me. Not threaten to dislocate his fingers if he "accidentally" brushed my ass while I was dropping off drinks at his table.

It wasn't about being touched. It was about consent. And a guy tracing his hands over every inch of your body with consent was sexy. Random, drunken ass grabs were not.

"Since you're ready to go, why don't you head downstairs. I'll be down as soon as I get my hair figured out and drop my tip log in the safe."

"You know he's taking the next few days off, so that could wait until tomorrow."

"I know," I sighed. While under normal circumstances Hudson was meticulous about his bookkeeping, he was scheduled to be gone until Monday. He'd earned a break with all the extra hours he'd been pulling. And I knew he typically withdrew when he was stressed, but I was worried about him. "He needs it after this week."

Even if I didn't talk to him most days, just knowing he was in the same building was comforting.

"I swear to God, if she's down there when we go down, I can't be responsible for *accidentally* spilling something on her. Preferably something disgusting that stains. I'm sure the cooks would help me find something."

"I love your petty side," I laughed, shooing her out of my bedroom with a flick of my wrist. "Try to hold in your vengeance until I'm there to help."

But if I had anything to do with it, she'd be getting more than a stained costume. If I had my way, she'd never step foot in this building again.

"Wish me luck." She spun in a circle, her short skirt twirling around her waist. "I'm in the mood to ruin my lipstick with a cute college boy."

"Same." But I wasn't imagining being kissed by a college guy. I was fantasizing about finally getting kissed by the one guy I couldn't have.

Chapter
Seven

Hudson

*J*UST PUT IT ON. *Put on the mask and take a deep breath. You got this. This is what she wants. You'll chase her, take her back to your place, and remind her how good you can be together.*

And then what? One hot night and she'd agree to work things out? Putting on this mask wouldn't be a band-aid, and as I stared at it peeking out the top of my backpack, a sense of unease swept over me.

"What are you still doing in here?"

I jumped at the voice coming from the office doorway.

"I thought you were out there trying to pick up women with bad boy issues?" Reid still hadn't put on a shirt. Instead, he was casually leaning against the doorframe with his helmet tucked under his arm, and I suddenly wished I had half the amount of swagger he had.

Judging by the loud music and voices coming from the other side of the building, the party had gotten into full swing while I'd been hiding in my office. I hadn't meant to stall joining the chaos, but since no one from the door had been sent to tell me Viv was here, I'd used the time to catch up on paperwork. It'd been so long since I'd had to think about trying to catch a woman's interest that I'd forgotten how. And I was having some major performance anxiety.

"Which you should be doing too," he laughed. "But it seems like you're in here having some existential crisis dressed all in black, like you're about to rob the place, instead of out there being charming so you can finally hook up with someone who doesn't want to change you."

Now that things were shaky between Viv and me, he hadn't hesitated to make his opinion of her known. Deep down, I knew how much he disliked her, mostly because she didn't seem to respect my decisions, but he didn't know her like I did.

She was smart, and passionate, and when we met, she'd been reckless and thirsty for adventure like I once had been.

"What exactly are you supposed to be? A black cloud?"

It felt like one was hovering over me right now. "No, this isn't the whole costume," I said, gesturing toward the rest of it.

"Ah, I see you took my comments about masked men to heart. Maybe you're looking for a bit of action from a girl with bad boy issues tonight, too. I just hope you don't pursue the wrong one."

I hoped that too.

"Just let me get this deposit put in the safe and I'll come find you."

"You better. Because as scary as it is, I'm making it my duty to be the voice of reason tonight. I think you need a wingman more than I do."

He might be right, but...

"Hey, is he in there?" A familiar voice asked from the hallway. My heart started beating faster, a sweat breaking out on the back of my neck.

"Yeah, he's getting ready, but I can give him those if you want."

"Thanks. I appreciate it," Charley responded, and I watched as she handed over a stack of receipts and her part of the tip share. She was mostly concealed by the doorframe, and part of me wanted to interrupt so I could see what she'd decided to wear to the party, but she wasn't the woman I should be focusing on right now.

Last year she'd been a sexy devil, and I remembered forcing myself to keep my eyes away from her the entire night, because thinking about how hot she looked was definitely not respecting my relationship with Viv, or her place as Hazel's friend.

"Make good choices out there," he teased, stroking his thumb over the back of her hand. "Don't let someone who doesn't deserve you charm you out of those tiny shorts."

"You seem to be mistaking me with someone else," she giggled, pushing a fingertip into his chest. "We both know I'm going to be the one charming some unsuspecting undergrad out of his costume at the end of the night."

"Come find me if you need me to scare off any creeps." His hand covered the back of hers where it rested on his bare skin, and an irrational flare of jealousy licked up my spine.

"I can handle myself just fine, but there's an angel out there that might need your services."

His eyes cut from the concealed woman in the hallway to me, his eyebrows lifting. I wasn't sure who she was talking about, but a text coming from my pocket distracted me.

> Mikey: Viv is here. Look for the dyed pigtails and pink boots.

Reid frowned at me, shaking his head, like he knew exactly what the message on my phone screen said. "Go have fun, Char. I think I'm gonna have my hands full dragging Hudson out of this office and forcing him to relearn what having fun is."

"Good luck with that," she laughed, and I closed my eyes as I tried to calm my nerves.

"You're the one who has control of what happens tonight." He crossed the room, shoving Charley's tips into my hand, and bending his knees slightly until I looked him in the eyes. "So don't fuck it up. Just because something is comfortable doesn't mean it's right. You don't have anything to prove to anyone but yourself."

"Thanks for the pep talk," I said sarcastically, and he narrowed his eyes as he pointed across the room.

"Put that mask on and go find someone who deserves that side of you." He turned on his heel, storming through my open door without a backward glance. I knew he was trying to be supportive, but I wasn't even sure what I deserved right now.

Hadn't I been a shitty boyfriend?

Didn't I have something to prove to Viv?

I wasn't sure what the right answer was, but I crossed the room and pulled the mask from the bag, running my thumb over the elongated black shape that was supposed to be a mouth.

"Don't fuck this up, dipshit," I muttered to myself and pulled it over my head, tucking the fabric into the open collar of my hoodie with shaking hands.

It was time to stop playing it safe.

Chapter Eight

Charley

BY THE TIME I'D turned in my tips, the building was a madhouse. There were people spilling down the side hallway where the bathrooms were located, already half drunk and out to cause some mischief. And I was about to join them.

I should have seen her coming from a mile away, but when the bite of someone's nails cut into my forearm, I jerked in their direction, ready to forget I was technically off the clock and kick their ass out of the bar.

"What the fuck are you supposed to be?" she yelled, stepping forward and crowding me against the wall.

I knew there was the possibility of seeing her tonight, but I hadn't thought she'd actually show up. Reid had given me as many details as Hudson had confessed to him, but one thing had been clear. Viv dumped Hudson, but gave him the old, "I want to stay friends" line to keep him on the hook.

Her eyes looked freaky, with her face covered in white face paint, large diamonds adorning her cheeks in metallic paint. She clearly hadn't gotten the memo that this was a *masked* costume party, but I wouldn't have recognized her immediately if it weren't for her piercing blue eyes. They were icy like her soul, and one of the only things that kept me from looking too much like her.

"Why does it matter what I am?" I asked, taking in the rest of her plastered-on costume.

She was wearing a red leather jacket, a tight white t-shirt splattered with fake blood, and tiny, glittery shorts that looked more like a bikini bottom with a leather belt at the top. Torn fishnet stockings disappeared into her hot pink boots, and a spiked dog collar completed the look.

"Because right now you look like the Wish version of my costume, and I want to know why you'd even dress up like this, knowing I was coming to the party with Hudson as my date in a coordinating one."

"Hudson is planning on wearing some sparkly panties like yours?" I laughed, enjoying the way her lips curled. It was so easy to get her riled up. She may have frightened Hazel, but she didn't intimidate me. "You sure he has the legs to pull that off?"

"No, you idiot. He's coming as the Joker. I dropped off the costume at his house earlier and texted him to meet me here. But I haven't heard from him all day. You must have seen his costume, and decided to come up with whatever this is to try to look like *you* were coming to the party with him."

While the idea of doing something to fuck with her was appealing, I'd had this costume planned for a while. Since Harley's misunderstood character was a kindred spirit, I'd wanted to honor that part of myself. But I didn't want to look like an actual clown to do it. Unlike some people. And the thought of carrying around a bat all night was appealing.

"As far as I know, he hasn't been home for the past few nights."

She growled, and my eyes widened as she pushed her hand into the middle of my chest. "And where the fuck has he been?"

"Why do you even care? I thought you broke up with him. Shouldn't you be at the party in town at the martini bar trying to catch a sugar daddy?"

"Stay the fuck away from him," she hissed, poking me with her fake nails on each word.

I didn't understand why she thought I was such a threat to her. Hudson had known me twice as long as her, and he'd chosen her. He clearly still saw me as his baby sister's best friend, and I'd come to terms with it. Maybe having a bit of distance would help me resolve my crush.

"Go home, Viv. No one wants you here. I think you've made your point that you can slum it, but we both know you're just a vapid bitch."

"Excuse me?"

Lifting the hot pink bat that was part of my costume, I pushed her back with my knee and smacked it against my palm. I was done letting her bully me, in her attempt to get the scoop on Hudson. She'd lost that privilege. They weren't together anymore, and I didn't let anyone talk to me like this.

"Go home, Viv. I'm not sure how that's a hard concept to grasp."

"Or what?" she shrieked, pushing her talons into my shoulder again.

"Or I'm gonna shove this bat up your..." I growled, but a body shoved in between us, pushing Viv further out into the hallway as I flattened against the wall.

Reid's familiar back tattoos calmed me down briefly, but I still wasn't ready to let her just walk all over everyone.

"Calm down, Killer," he teased, flashing me a smile through the open mask of his motorcycle helmet. "I'll get her out of here. You go have fun."

"But..." I wanted to be the one to kick her ass out the door.

"Seriously, go. You know Hudson wouldn't want you to make a scene."

"Where is he?" Viv shrieked, fighting against Reid's outstretched hand while he attempted to block her from getting close to me.

"None of your fucking business," he growled, turning back in her direction. He reached behind himself, pushing me toward the direction of the bar, and urged her in the opposite direction. "You lost the right to know that."

He disliked her nearly as much as I did, so I knew he'd make her leave or get her to calm down enough to behave herself.

Swinging the bat in my hand, I took a deep breath and re-centered myself. I wasn't here to deal with Viv. I had a mission of my own for tonight.

THERE WAS SOMETHING THRILLING about walking through a dark room full of strangers while wearing a mask.

Every single person in this room was playing a part tonight.

I hadn't decided what mine would be yet.

Adrenaline for the unknown thrummed through my veins as I scanned the room, watching the other anonymous partygoers drop into their chosen roles for the night.

The giggling sorority girls dressed as sexy woodland creatures crowded around a high-top table, batting their fake eyelashes at a table of college baseball players nearby. They went with the super original ploy and wore their uniforms as costumes.

The more *alt* crowd was dressed in various macabre costumes of witches and ghouls, meant to warn people away from them doing their own type of mating dance.

I looked over and saw my very *angelic* best friend—who was not acting very angelic—flirting with a man dressed as a devil at one of the tables bordering the dance floor. As I continued to scan the room, my eyes stopped on a shirtless man wearing a motorcycle helmet as he watched her from over his *conquest-for-the-night's* head. Reid had gotten rid of Viv faster than I'd expected. And was clearly planning to act as Haz's protector for the night.

My plan with Hazel had been to stick together for the night, but as her hand covered the man's standing across from her, I had a feeling I'd be the third wheel in their conversation. I'd excused myself as soon as I'd left my bat at the table—still disappointed that I wasn't allowed to use it to wipe the sneer off Vivienne's face.

My costume was inspired by who I liked to think of as my alter ego. She was strong, unapologetic, sexy and independent. Even if she was a bit unhinged. Tonight, I wanted to function outside the constraints that life had put upon me.

I wanted to be wild.

I wanted to be sensual.

I wanted to forget who I couldn't have and let someone else make me feel desirable. Reckless.

I *wanted* to get fucked by one of these masked men.

The question was, which one?

Letting my eyes track the people surrounding me, I headed toward the apex of the crowd, my body heating as the bodies thickened near the dance floor, the music vibrating through my limbs.

Stretching my hands above my head, I let the beat flow through me, swaying my hips as couples gyrated around me. Sexual energy pulsed in the air, flowing freely as I closed my eyes and just let the feeling of anticipation build.

"Not paying attention to your surroundings when you look this tempting is dangerous," a low voice growled near my ear as a large hand traced the exposed skin of my side and settled on my stomach, pulling until my back settled against a warm body. Inhaling, I knew who was touching me, and I leaned my head back into his strong chest, tucking my face against his neck.

"Touching a woman without her consent when she's wearing boots with a three-inch heel is dangerous," I replied, enjoying the way his fingers flexed, digging into my skin.

"Such a fierce little creature." His voice was raspy, and if I hadn't spent hours surrounded by him, I would have had trouble placing it. But I knew that voice, and I knew that scent, and I knew that I had to be hallucinating because there was no way Hudson knew he was touching me.

"You have no idea what I'm capable of."

As the music changed, a seductive beat flowed through the bar—charging the air with sexual tension—and Hudson stepped even closer, shoving a strong thigh between my legs, erasing any space between us as he started to move.

Closing my eyes again, I raised my arms again, letting the rhythm of the song carry me. His strong hands gripped my waist, anchoring me to him as his hips followed my movements, swaying and grinding until I was breathless. I always sensed the hidden sexual attraction between the two of us, but I never anticipated how it would truly feel to have his hands on me. Gripping my stomach, tracing up my sides, his fingers interlocking with mine before he spun me around to face him.

"Look at me."

That low raspy voice would be the death of me, my eyelids reluctantly fluttering open to connect with the deep brown of his, the dimness of the room doing nothing to conceal the heat of his gaze.

His eyes locked with mine through the ominous slits in his mask, and a thrill ran up my spine. He was looking at me like he wanted to devour me. Like I'd fantasized about him looking at me countless times while I lay upstairs in my bed, my hands between my legs and my eyes tightly closed.

"Fucking sinful," he groaned, leaning forward. If he wasn't wearing that ridiculous mask, I had no doubt his full lips would've been tracing the skin on my jaw. "Such a naughty fucking girl looking like this. You wanted to tempt me to do bad things, didn't you?"

His hands grasped my ass, pulling me forward into him, my pulse spiking as I felt his hard cock through his jeans. Never once in my life had I expected that I would be capable of making Hudson Rivera this hard, but now I craved it.

I wanted to feel it...

stroke it...

lick it...

suck it...

choke on it...

rub it against my cheek...

But more than anything, I wanted to see it. See the physical proof that he might find me as attractive as I found him. That he might want me a fraction of how much I'd wanted him for years. The yearning that'd been barely concealed for all these years rushed through me, manifesting in this primal need to mark him.

Wrapping my arms around his waist, I skimmed my palms underneath the back of his hoodie, digging my nails into his overheated flesh, relishing the groan that vibrated against my neck.

"Be careful, not sure you'll like what happens when you provoke me."

But I would. Even though this interaction was completely unexpected, and I had a feeling he thought I was someone else, I wanted to make him snap.

Scraping the nails I'd painted bright pink earlier against the center of his back, I gasped when his fingers dug into my shorts, gripping me—almost painfully, but pushing me toward so much pleasure—as he moaned against my shoulder. The plastic of his mask scratched my cheek, and I had no idea how he wasn't burning up in his costume, but a plan was formulating to get him out of it. As soon as possible.

"Take me somewhere quieter," I demanded, flattening my lips against the scratchy material of the black hood holding his mask in place. "Please."

"Since when are you in charge?" he chuckled, loosening his hold and grasping my hand. "But since you asked so nicely..."

Stumbling to catch up with him, I clutched his fingers tightly as he led me through the crowd toward the back hallway. It was the opposite side of the building from where Viv had confronted me, and hopefully she was long gone.

This side was the same back hallway that I had caught couples nearly fucking in countless times, annoyed that people couldn't wait until they got somewhere more private. But now I understood their desperation. As we passed the back staircase that led up to my apartment, my fingers twitched as I debated dragging him into my bed instead of following whatever plans he had for me.

But I didn't want to second guess what was happening. Because this might be the only time I was the sole focus of Hudson's desire. I didn't want to lead tonight. I wanted to follow. I wanted him to chase. I wanted to feel like I was the center of his attention. The thing he couldn't resist. He'd started this, not me, and knowing it'd piss off the bitch who thought she still had control over him just added to the excitement.

Suddenly, he stopped, pulling me into the alcove of his closed office door, and grasping my other hand, stretching them above my head and pinning my wrists to the wall with a single hand.

"Cute shirt, naughty girl," he rasped, his gaze tracing across the words emblazoned across the cotton. I'd opted for a short-sleeved raglan T-shirt with pink sleeves and a tight pair of cut-off shorts.

"Mommy's. Little. Devil." The words were low and drawn out in this deeper voice he'd adapted, the pitch making the hairs on the back of my neck stand. "I thought your shirt was supposed to say *Daddy's Little Monster?*"

I shrugged as much as I could with my arms pinned above my head. The excitement of this unexpected role play had me wanting to play along, and I pitched my voice lower, trying to make it sound sultrier. "Don't have a *Daddy* to be a monster for. You throwing your hat in the ring for the part?"

"You'd like that. Wouldn't you? Trying to act out for me. But maybe *I'm* the monster you should be looking out for."

"You don't scare me, Hu..." My words cut off with a gasp as I almost said his name. "You don't have it in you."

"We'll see about that."

The grip on my wrists tightened briefly before he released me, stepping back. But before I could move, his palms were gripping my hips and spinning me toward the hallway, his large palm gripping the back of my neck between my swaying pigtails. Leading me to the back door that led to the alley where he stored his bike, Hudson reached around me to open it.

The temperature had dropped since I'd gotten home from class earlier, the crisp late fall air biting into the exposed skin my tiny costume didn't cover. I shivered and his fingers tightened, sending a rush of adrenaline through my system. I wanted to say it was the cold that had my nipples standing at attention, but it was the commanding way he marched me to the edge of the parking lot, halting where the gravel ended and the darkened woods at the edge of town loomed beyond.

A gasp escaped me, my breath condensing in a mist as it floated toward the trees. I trembled as he eased the grip on the back of my neck, his rough palm tracing forward to grip my throat.

"Not so tough now, are you?"

Without the chaotic noise of the dance floor inside to mask it, the ominous tone I'd never heard from him made goosebumps race up my arms. Whatever game he was playing, I was fully into it.

"Fuck you."

His grip tightened, and with anyone else, I would have been nervous to put myself into a vulnerable position like this, but when a deep hum—almost a growl—built in his throat, I knew playing along was the right move.

"Mmm. Maybe later, if you're good. Now I want you to do something for me. Are you listening?"

"Mmhmm," I hummed, anticipation coursing through me.

"Run, little devil. Run."

The mouth uttering the words was familiar, but the tone was not. Hudson's typically subdued voice was strong and assertive. There wasn't an ounce of hesitation in his command, and my eyes widened as he stepped away from me, beginning to count.

"10...9...8..."

Chapter Nine

"**B**ETTER GET GOING BEFORE you run out of time."

She hesitated, her fingers twitching as I stepped backward, moving myself away from her tempting body. I hadn't remembered her feeling so good in my arms.

"7... I don't see you moving. It's like you don't even want to play."

This was her idea, and now that she was having her moment, she was freezing.

"6... You're not making this very fun. I thought you wanted some excitement."

That seemed to snap her out of whatever trance she was in, and I watched her teal tipped pigtails sway as she darted into the trees.

Blood rushed in my ears as I slowly followed, my breath almost oppressive against the plastic of the mask. This thing was fucking hot, but it wasn't as unbearable with the cooler temperature outside.

Inside, on the packed dance floor, surrounded by people, I'd been almost claustrophobic, especially when she'd wrapped her arms around me and scratched her nails down my back. She'd never done that before. And the sudden sharp bite of pain it ignited sent a thrill through me. I wanted—no, I *needed*—her to do it again.

The leaves crunched under my sneakers, a cool wind howling in the distance as it crossed the ravine where a creek separated the town from the plot of land my family owned along the edge of the city limits.

A sense of unease rushed through me as I realized if she wasn't careful, and turned off the trail ahead, that she could go plummeting down a thirty-foot drop to the shallow water before I could reach her.

"I thought you were chasing me." Her playful voice carried through the breeze, and I turned toward it, letting the tension ease and the adrenaline kick in.

"5..." I shouted, a thrill running through me as a shriek sounded from not too far away.

"4..."

"You're slow as fuck!" she giggled, and part of me was happy that she was seeming to enjoy this game. I'd been so worried earlier that this was a terrible idea. That I'd do something wrong or say something wrong and drive her away forever.

"3..."

A twig snapped from behind a tree a few yards off the trail to my right and I paused, listening for signs of her.

Squinting through the eye holes in my mask, I saw a flash of pink from the bottom of her boots. The moonlight reflected off the white mask obscuring half her face. She looked almost ethereal, peeking around from behind the large trunk, squeaking when she saw me standing closer than she clearly expected and covering her mouth before she ducked out of sight again.

"2... You're really terrible at hiding from me."

She giggled again, and I followed the peals of laughter, stalking off the trail and watching for flashes of pink as I picked up my pace.

"1... Here I come..."

A small hand darted out from behind a tree as I passed it, and she pushed me up against the trunk, a grunt escaping my mouth as she looked up at me.

"Not yet," she whispered, pressing her body against mine, flattening her palm against the front of my jeans. "But I bet you will be soon."

The little minx had turned the tables on me, and I wasn't mad about it. She squeezed, a rush of pain coursing through me at her tight grip, immediately followed by a release of endorphins when a feeling took over my body I'd never felt before.

We had some intense sex over the years, but the buildup before had never left this intense of a primal need to claim her.

"You didn't try very hard to get away from me. Weren't you scared that the stranger following you into the woods was going to do something bad to you?"

Her eyes locked onto mine, holding me in place as her fingers fumbled with my belt, unbuckling it and tugging down my zipper. I throbbed against the material of my boxer briefs, aching for her to touch me.

"Maybe I wanted to do something bad to him instead."

She hadn't told me about this part of the fantasy. I hadn't even known she could be this playfully dominant. She'd always let me take the lead, be the pursuer, the one who initiated things, the one who was on top. The one who was in control.

"And what do you want to do to him?"

She smirked, her lips visible at the edge of her mask, and I watched with rapt attention as she bit the side of her bottom lip, tugging the plump flesh briefly before her fingers crept through the hole in the flap, fingers wrapping around my hot skin.

"He's about to find out..."

"Mmhmm," I hummed, leaning my head back against the rough bark of the tree. The thick fabric of my black hood protected me from it, but part of me wanted to feel the bite of it against my scalp as she touched me. To embrace the pain mixed with the pleasure she brought with her touch.

"But he'll have to catch me first."

Her fingers tugged roughly one more time before she blew a sassy little air kiss and turned on her heels. She bolted through the wooded area surrounding us with surprising speed for someone wearing such high heels.

Deciding to double down on playing her little game, I carefully zipped my pants and stalked around the large tree she'd disappeared behind, listening for sounds of movement in the distance.

I tried to keep my footfalls quiet, my heart pounding while I tracked her movements, listening as she zigzagged through the trees, trying to anticipate her next move. She'd been right. The thrill of the chase was fun. And now I could see the appeal of switching things up every once in a while.

The longer it took to catch her, the more the adrenaline raced through my veins, building for when I finally caught up with her. The sinister part of me wanted to punish her for teasing me. For wrapping her little, soft hand around me and making me desperate to fuck her.

I wanted to push her to her knees and violate her mouth, relishing in the gagging sounds I knew she'd make as she swallowed my cock.

Pausing, I waited behind a nearby tree, listening to the rustling of leaves coming closer and closer. She sounded out of breath as she crept through a clearing a few feet away, and I balled my fists at my sides to keep myself from giving away my position.

From my fixed position, her body came into view. The full hunter's moon seemed so close, the illumination casting an ominous orange glow across the space between us and giving away her proximity as she crept through the trees and shrubs. The way she moved was mesmerizing. How her toned legs flexed as she carefully planned her footfalls. The way her tight, cropped t-shirt heaved every time she took a labored breath. The flushed skin on her neck.

I wasn't sure if it was from the cold or the excitement, but I was about to make it redder when I wrapped my hand around her delicate throat.

She wanted the fantasy, and I was determined to see this through. To try to be what she needed.

Deliberately keeping my footsteps silent, I stalked behind her, careful to keep myself concealed in the shadows. It was intoxicating knowing what I had planned for her once I caught her. She may have teased me and then turned the tables, but we had plenty of time for me to take the lead.

She paused, bracing her hands on a large tree trunk, and carefully peering around the side to look for signs of me.

Only a short step away, a branch cracked beneath my foot, and I saw her flinch, her body gearing up to flee. But I was faster, my hand shooting out and wrapping around her throat.

"Not so fast, little devil. I believe we have some unfinished business." She shuddered at the low, menacing tone I wasn't aware I was capable of until this moment. And I wondered if her heart was beating as fast as mine.

"What? No sassy little comebacks for me now? I thought you enjoyed testing my patience?"

My fingers tightened as I flattened my chest against her back, urging her forward until she was a hair's breadth away from being pushed against the rough bark in front of her face. Even if I was wildly turned on, and bordering on losing control, I never wanted to hurt her.

"I..." she squeaked as I pulled her head back roughly, leaning down so I could whisper directly in her ear.

The plastic of the mask pressed against the hair on my chin, making a crackling sound as I pushed my lips as close to her skin as I could.

"Too late now. I've got something else for those lips to do."

Her body shook as I held her captive, and I hoped I wasn't scaring her, but I was too far gone to worry about it at this point.

"On your knees."

Loosening my hold on her neck, I moved my hand to her shoulder, gripping firmly as I urged her to the mossy brush next to the tree.

I should have taken off my hoodie and laid it on the ground to protect her knees, but the devil on my shoulder wanted to see the scrapes on them later. I wanted the reminder of this moment manifested on her skin like a brand.

"Hu..." she gasped as I used my hand to spin her, forcing her to her knees at my feet and stepping forward until the back of her head pressed against the trunk of the tree. Her blonde pigtails and stark white mask gleamed in the moonlight breaking through the canopy overhead, and she almost would have looked angelic if it wasn't for the way she was biting her lip.

"You wanted to play with it earlier. Now's your chance. *Take. Out. My. Cock.*" My demand ended in a rough growl, watching what expression I could see from behind her mask turn to one of anticipation.

It'd been years since she treated sucking my cock like it was an event to look forward to, and I wasn't wasting this opportunity.

Grasping one long pigtail in my fist, I yanked her forward, pressing her nose into the front of my jeans, my cock throbbing behind the material.

"You made me this hard. Now fucking take care of it."

Her fingers shook as she unzipped my zipper, my belt clinking as she tugged the material down. Her nails scratched my thighs as she slipped her fingers underneath the waistband of my boxers and pulled them down, my cock bobbing in her face.

"Open," I urged, using her pigtail as leverage and I groaned as she obeyed, her lips parting and the head slipping between them. "Fuck..."

"Mmm," she hummed and swirled her tongue around the head. She dragged her nails down my thighs, digging them into my skin as she rocked forward, eliciting a pained gasp from me as her teeth dragged down my length.

"Be. Fucking. Nice." I growled, flipping my wrist to wrap her pigtail around my palm, using it as leverage to pull her back until my cock was poised just out of reach from her lips.

"No," she whispered. "This cock doesn't deserve nice. It doesn't *want* me to be nice. And neither do you."

"Fuck," I grunted as she swallowed me whole, gagging as I rammed against the back of her throat.

I tried...

I fucking tried not to thrust and risk hurting her, but when her nails dug in further, I couldn't hold back.

"Oh, we want to play games now?" I groaned, thrusting forward in quick succession, watching the moonlight highlight the spit trickling down her chin. I could barely see her eyes watering from behind her mask as she gagged and groaned around me.

Typically, I was thrilled when a woman wanted to give me head, so I was respectfully grateful instead of being a mindless animal, but the way she forced her head forward every time I tried to pull her back to breathe had me quickly chasing down what I knew would be the mother of all orgasms.

It didn't help that when I closed my eyes, breaking her intense eye contact, I was picturing the filthy sound I knew it'd make if she choked on my cum.

My cock pulsed against her tongue, and I gritted my teeth to hold back, trying to prolong this intense ecstasy mixed with the agony at the brutal way I was fucking her face.

The sound of rough breaths escaping her nose mixed with the filthy wet, slurping and gagging noises accompanying them pushed me right over the edge and I thrust forward, my neck arching back and a pained groan echoing through the trees as I filled her dirty little mouth.

As soon as the pulses ceased, I released her hair, flexing my hand and watching as she tried to catch her breath once my cock slipped from her glistening red lips. Lips I wanted to kiss, lips I wanted to fuck again and then watch with rapt attention while cum dribbled from in between them.

Once her breathing had evened out, I gripped her chin, using my thumb to smear the moisture on her chin over her bottom lip.

"I'm gonna fuck this again," I promised. "But that can wait. It's your turn."

Excitement flared in her eyes, her tongue flicking out to swipe across the pad of my thumb, eliciting another pained groan from me. My spent cock twitched, and I had a feeling the way she looked on her knees—lips glistening with my cum while her chest heaved from the exertion of gagging herself on my cock—would dramatically reduce my refractory period, but I reluctantly stepped away and tucked myself back into my boxer briefs.

She watched with hungry eyes as I zipped up my jeans and fastened my belt, using my fingers to motion for her to stand from where she was still perched on her knees. Continuing the nonverbal commands, I repeated the motion, nodding when she stood—leaves still plastered to her knees—and spinning my finger to indicate she should turn to face the tree behind her.

Her shoulders trembled as I slowly advanced on her, tucking my face in close to her neck as my chest brushed against her back. "You might want to hold on."

Chuckling as her hands shot out without hesitation, her hot pink fingernails were a stark contrast to the dark bark underneath her fingers.

"Mmmm," I whispered, tracing the back of my hand against the soft skin of her stomach as I reached for the button on her tiny shorts. Unfastening it with a flick of my fingertips, I tried to let some of the menace out of my voice. "You're trembling. Is it from excitement, or are you cold?"

She hesitated, but as I watched her breath puff out into the cold air in front of her, I had my answer.

"Stay," I commanded, stepping back far enough to unzip my hoodie, shrugging it off as I watched her fingers flex anxiously against the tree trunk. Crowding against her again, I grasped one of her hands, slipping the soft material around her, placing her palm back against the bark and repeating the motion on the other side. "Now spread your legs."

She widened her stance, pushing her ass into me as I wrapped my hands around her hips. "Don't hold back when I make you come, because I want to hear you fucking scream."

Chapter

Ten

Charley

M Y SEXUAL HISTORY WASN'T exactly vanilla, dipping into the kinkier side of life when I dated the occasional dominant man. It'd been thrilling to consent to giving over control, so seeing this side of Hudson had me feeling almost feral.

He was clearly taking the reins on things, only briefly letting me tease him before he took back the dominant position. I had no idea he was like this. If I'd known, my determination to push down my attraction to him would have crumbled a long time ago. The last time he'd been single, I'd still been in college.

If I'd initiated things back then, would he have even given me the time of day? Would I have been ready to embrace this side of him?

"You liked having my cock in your mouth, didn't you?" The rough plastic of his mask scraped against my neck, and I shuddered against him, overwhelmed by his much larger body.

His sweatshirt was warm, the long sleeves now protecting my palms from the rough bark of the tree, but it didn't protect me from the rough skin on his fingertips rasping across my stomach.

"I bet your panties are soaked. I can't wait to feel you dripping all over me when you come, your tight pussy milking my fingers like I know it wants to milk my cock," he murmured, roughly pressing his hand into the denim of my shorts, forcing my zipper into my bare skin. Instinctively, I rocked my hips forward into the friction and gasped as the rough denim grazed my clit. To say I was turned on was probably putting it lightly, but this was his show, and I was just along for the ride.

The heel of his palm rocked into my movements, more whimpers escaping my mouth. He seemed to feed on the sounds I was making, grinding his hips into me from behind.

"These noises are driving me crazy. I've never heard you this desperate before. Are you ready for me to make you come?"

"Yes," I gasped, leaning back tightly against him as he unbuttoned my shorts with one hand, slowly drawing the zipper down.

His hand disappeared beneath the material, and he paused as his fingers traced my skin. "You're fucking bare," he growled, his rough fingertips slipping effortlessly against my wet flesh. My pussy throbbed against him, already so overstimulated it wouldn't take much to set me off. "You knew this would drive me nuts, didn't you?"

I didn't. Since I obviously had no way to anticipate tonight's events. Although, he may have been a fleeting thought as I lay with my eyes clenched shut, trying to picture my happy place while my waxer worked her magic.

My body hummed as his fingers played in the only tiny strip of neatly trimmed hair left. "You've never waxed for me before. I want to feel you like this all the time. Once I get you to where we're going later, I'm going to bury my face in this soft cunt and never come up for air."

"Oh God," I whimpered, trying to stay in character as his fingers slipped lower, tracing the bare skin between my thighs before slowly pushing inside, not stopping until he reached the place that had me squirming and moaning in his arms. "Fuck. Right there. Don't stop."

"Don't plan to," he rasped, twisting and turning his fingertips while he fucked me with his hand. His motions were almost desperate, harsh pants echoing through the mask he was still wearing and fanning across the skin of my neck. "Want to make you feel as good as you made me feel."

"So good," I murmured, clenching my eyes closed as I felt the approaching orgasm bearing down on me.

"Fuck. I wish I could see you better. This fucking mask is keeping me from kissing you the way I want to. I want to feel your skin against my teeth. Scrape them down your throat. Bite your perky nipples until they're red. Watch your face while I devour this pussy."

"Oh, shit. I'm gonna come," I whimpered, and he pulled me back roughly, shoving his fingers deep and curling them until I saw stars, my legs almost giving out with the force of the climax that rushed through my body.

"That's it, baby. Fuck my hand, draw it out."

Squirming against him, I thrust my hips, fighting against the onslaught—completely overstimulated—but he wasn't going to let me go. And I didn't want him to.

"Breathe. Just breathe. Can you feel another building? I don't think you're done yet," he coaxed, chuckling darkly as I tried to break free of his hold. The insistent thrust of his fingers was over-stimulating, but I was so wet I'd already soaked his hand. "I can feel it. I can feel you desperate to come again. Should I let you finish?"

"Yes—*fuck*," I broke off in a gasp as I jackknifed forward, my cheek scratching against the bark of the tree while I violently came, my entire body shaking.

"Fuck yes," he groaned, slowing his movements and slowly drawing his wet fingers out of my shorts, trailing them under the hem of my tight crop top. "And the next time you come for me; I'm going to have my mouth all over these. I bet you'd like me to fuck them. Wouldn't you?"

I nodded, panting as stars flashed across my field of vision. Hudson had made me come faster and harder than any other guy that I had ever been with. And we hadn't even had sex yet. Was I going to pass out when he fucked me? The thought was thoroughly appealing.

"Wouldn't you?" he growled, his fingers delving beneath the lace cups of my bra and pinching my nipple roughly.

"Yes."

"And I bet you'd like it if I couldn't control myself. If it was so good that I couldn't hold back and covered you in my release. I'm looking forward to seeing this pale skin splattered in my cum. You'd look so depraved and pretty and hungry for me to fuck you."

I had no idea where he was coming up with this stuff, because his mouth was utterly filthy. How could she ever walk away from him when he was capable of something like this?

Fuck.

My heart raced as a fleeting thought took hold of me.

What if he thought he was with *her* right now? What if Hudson thought I was Viv?

Part of me was a little disgusted at the thought I could ever be mistaken for her. But it was dark inside the bar tonight. And on a normal day we eerily resembled each other. Almost identical height, same color hair—even though I took up dying mine every color of the rainbow when he started dating her—we even sounded alike. The only real difference was that my eyes were hazel and hers were an almost translucent blue.

Reid had commented to me more than once that it was a little freaky that we looked nearly identical but were polar opposites. I'd always thought that was why Hudson would never be interested in me.

My personality wasn't what he was looking for. I wasn't his type. Maybe I still wasn't.

"Are you okay?" he whispered, stroking his thumb along the edge of my breast, making me shudder against him.

"I'm fine," I whispered. But I wasn't fine.

Should I stop this? Should I take off this mask and turn around? See if he still wanted to take this further knowing for certain it was me?

"No, you're not," he murmured, nuzzling my cheek. "You're cold. Do you want me to stop?"

I shook my head, leaning back against him, sniffling. "Keep going."

He nodded, holding me tighter before his voice dropped back into character.

"Such a good *fucking* girl. Coming all over me. I think you enjoyed that. Letting a stranger fuck your sweet pussy with his hand after you sucked his dick. So deliciously naughty. Tell me how naughty you are…" He pulled his hand out of my shirt, wrapping his fingers around my throat. It wasn't cutting off my air, but I liked the possessive press of his fingers against my jaw. "Now."

"I'm…" I moaned as he pressed his hips against me, already hard again. I gasped, closing my eyes as I leaned back into his tight hold. "Naughty…"

Grunting, his arms tightened almost painfully around me, my jaw aching as he gripped me. "Yes, you fucking are. So bad. But now I've had a taste of you, and I don't plan on letting you go."

Before I could react, Hudson released me, stepping back slightly before he grasped my wrists, bringing them in front of my waist. "Hold still and I'll try not to hurt you."

The loud *rip* sound of a zip tie tightening startled me, and he let out a deep chuckle that made the hairs on the back of my neck stand.

"The way I see it, you have two options. You come with me nicely and be my little angel." His voice was low and firm, almost mocking as he said the words *nicely* and *angel*.

"Or I give you a head start to see if you can get away from me. But if I catch you, you're my naughty little devil for the night. Maybe even longer than that."

I already knew which one I was planning to choose. While being a pillow princess may have been his toxic ex's personality, it sure as hell wasn't fucking mine. Adrenaline flooded my system again, and the drowsiness of the orgasms he'd expertly rung out of me with his long, talented fingers faded into the periphery.

"So which one is it, are you naughty or nice? Because your choice will determine what else I put you through once I get you alone." And I couldn't fucking wait. If this was just a preview of what the rest of the night held, I was eager to get somewhere more private.

Not that the thought of him fucking me for real against the rough bark of a nearby tree didn't have its appeal, but I wanted to see all of him. And I wanted him to see all of *me*.

"Which one do *you* want?" I asked, my disguised voice stronger than I thought it'd be.

"I'm good with either. Both ways the end is going to be the same. I get inside this pussy and make you come until you can't handle it anymore. Then I'm going to fuck you hard until I fill you with my cum."

I didn't even hesitate to answer after that filthy promise. "Naughty…"

"That'a girl. So, for the rest of the night, the more you fight me, the more you get punished."

And I was all for punishment.

"And I'm going to *enjoy* punishing you."

Me too. Because he didn't know that I loved to be spanked. But he'd find out soon enough.

Chapter Eleven

Charley

ANTICIPATION RAN THROUGH ME as I waited to see what he'd do next. "You've got until I count to five, and then I'm coming after you. And I'm not going to let you get away this time."

"What happened to ten?" I teased, trying to turn, but he grabbed the back of my neck and pushed me forward until my cheek was millimeters from the tree in front of me.

"Don't fucking push me."

"But I think you like it when I do," I purred, leaning into the seductive vixen voice.

He growled, roughly yanking me to the side and aiming me toward the trail that led through the woods back to the bar. "You better fucking run."

This time, when he released me, I darted through the brush, my pounding heart the only thing I could hear.

Hudson's voice faded as I wove down the trail, and then suddenly it stopped when he finished counting. I knew why he only counted to five—he had no doubt he'd find me. Because I didn't want to get away.

Deciding to see exactly how much he'd punish me as a result, I quickly scanned to make sure there wasn't anyone loitering outside the back of the building before I screamed, trying to make myself sound panicked.

"Help! He's coming! Help please!"

The wind was knocked out of me as strong arms wrapped around my waist, Hudson pulling me tightly against his solid chest. His rough palm covered my mouth, and my panicked breaths fogged in the air in front of my face while he carried me toward the side of the building where he'd parked his car.

He rarely drove his car to work unless it was safer because of the weather, so it seemed like this little scenario of his had been planned.

A flare of jealousy burned through me at the thought he planned this for *her*, but then I grinned against his palm. Viv wasn't fucking here right now.

Fuck that demure, *psychotic*, little plastic doll, I was as chaotic as they came.

And I had no plans of stopping this. The harsh light of day might bring consequences I didn't want to face in the morning, but tonight...

Tonight, Hudson was mine.

"Don't bother screaming. The music is too loud for anyone to hear you," he warned as the hand covering my mouth loosened. "Stay quiet or I'm going to have to shut you up. Although, I think you enjoy having your mouth full."

Nodding, my chest heaved as I waited for him to move his hand away further.

When it dropped to his side, I lunged forward, letting out a loud scream, hoping there wasn't anyone outside the front door listening either. I didn't want Hudson to actually get arrested for kidnapping me, but I also wanted to see what he'd do.

"You asked for it." He let out a dark chuckle, banding a strong forearm across my exposed stomach, covering my mouth with a cloth, and quickly tying it tightly around the back of my head.

Hudson spun me around, his eyes wild as he looked down at me briefly before he bent and hefted me over his shoulder.

Yanking on his T-shirt, I scratched my nails across his lower back, trying not to giggle at the yelp and pained moan he let out. "Keep it up, little devil. Your time is coming."

If I could have, I would have told him to bring it on...but as I thrashed and kicked while he carried me off, I think he got the message.

My head spun as Hudson shoved me into the back seat of his car.

Again, I had the fleeting thought that with anyone else I'd be terrified, but as he leaned in over my body, gently making sure the cloth covering my mouth wasn't too tight, I'd never felt safer.

"Stay. Here. Don't move an inch." His tone was serious, but I could tell from the frantic scanning of my face, he was trying to make sure I was okay with this. "When I come back, if you've tried to escape, I'll know. If I can't trust you to behave when I need you to, I'll have to leave you here instead of taking you somewhere quiet to have my fun with you."

Nodding, I tried to calm my breathing, wordlessly assuring him that I'd be good...for now.

"I'll be back in a few minutes."

My ears rang in the silence of the car after he slammed the door.

Was he going to take me back to his house? Or somewhere else?

Either way, I needed to let Hazel know I was gone. I lifted my hips, shifting my arms to the side to wiggle my phone out of my back pocket. Thankfully, he had zip tied them in front of me instead of behind or I'd be stuck.

My fingers shook as I used my thumbs to type in the code to unlock the screen and open my text messages. Apparently facial recognition didn't work too well when you were wearing a mask and had a gag tied across your mouth.

> *Charley: Left with Hudson. Won't be home tonight. Be safe.*

The wind howled outside the car, but I didn't hear him out there. He must have gone back inside the building for something. I really hoped he didn't run into Vivienne in there, because I was looking forward to the rest of this role play. And that bitch wasn't spoiling this for either of us. Hudson deserved someone who actually *wanted* to be with him.

Before my thoughts could spiral with more worst-case scenarios, my phone buzzed in my hands.

> *Hazel: Same to you, but please DON'T call me with details later.*
> *There are things I don't need to know about my brother.*

I wanted to ask her how she knew something was going on she wouldn't want details for, but the sound of the bar door slamming had my fingers flying across the keys. Hazel had known about my crush on her brother for nearly as long as I'd had it. It was hard to keep things from someone who knew you as well as we knew each other. But even she didn't know how deeply my feelings for him had grown since I started working at the bar.

> *Charley: You're no fun.*

Her response was immediate.

> *Hazel: Please don't break his heart.*

I highly doubted that would happen any time soon. I'd have to be in possession of it to break it.

> *Charley: I'm more worried about mine.*

Hazel had encouraged me more than once to tell him how I felt, but with Viv in the picture, there was no way I'd put myself in the middle of their relationship and risk that kind of rejection. Having him as a friend was more important than my misplaced crush. Although I'd let her fascination with Reid stay concealed, even though I knew she had a thing for her brother's oldest friend. But I wasn't sure if her feelings for him were more than just physical.

Both older men were handsome, but I'd only ever had eyes for one of them. Seemed the Rivera siblings both might have the hots for their counterparts' besties. Well, hopefully, the older one would once he realized who he was with.

But what I'd told Hazel was true. I was more worried about my heart than his. He'd always seen me as this annoying little sister he needed to protect before tonight, and I wondered if that would change for him once he knew I was the woman he'd done all those things to a short while ago. Surely after what had transpired against that tree Hudson knew he wasn't with his ex.

Before I could delve any deeper into his motivations for chasing me through the woods in a mask to finger fuck me against a tree, the door to the driver's seat was wrenched open. Reflexively, I shoved my phone back in my pocket before he looked into the back seat and noticed I had it.

He'd really committed to the menacing masked man persona earlier—despite a few slips to make sure I was okay—and I didn't want to destroy the illusion by letting him know he'd left the zip ties too loose. If I wanted to, I could snap these in seconds and jump out of the car before he could leave, but I wasn't doing anything to upset the flow of things.

Because I knew Hudson, if he overthought this encounter, it'd stop. He didn't like confrontation, and he thrived on being in control. I only hoped that the control part would translate to the bedroom. Because whether it was a good idea or not, I was going to fuck my best friend's brother tonight.

It felt more like Christmas than Halloween, but I wasn't turning down the gift of dick regardless of the holiday. Especially not from the guy I'd had a crush on for a decade.

Chapter Twelve

Hudson

GLANCING OVER MY SHOULDER after I slammed the door, I exhaled in relief when I saw she hadn't moved from where I'd laid her down in the back seat. I knew it probably wasn't safe to drive without a seatbelt on her through the mountains at night, but we weren't going far. I would be careful.

The only thing I was worried about at this point was getting there before the weather front moved in. A light dusting of snow had already accumulated on my windshield as the temperature continued to drop. And judging by the large mass of blue and purple on my weather app, it was going to dump a lot of snow, and fast.

I'd taken supplies up once I'd finalized my plans earlier and made sure that there was enough gas to keep the generator running through the weekend if we lost power. She'd hated it the last time we'd spent the weekend at my family's cabin, but I was committed to making this kidnapping thing at least somewhat believable.

It was all a role play, because I'd be a fuck ton more nervous if I was actually kidnapping someone, but she'd seemed to love everything leading up to this moment.

Even though it was her idea, I'd anticipated her breaking character by now and insisting we go to her condo for the night. She was almost obsessed with her nightly routine, and I cursed when I realized I'd forgotten to bring the shower things she'd left at my house. She'd just have to deal with it for a night because I wasn't stopping now. Hopefully, we'd be too busy fucking for it to be an issue.

"Don't even think about trying to get away from me once I stop. Because there isn't anyone else for miles around where I'm taking you."

I didn't wait for a response, turning around and starting the car. The powerful engine roared to life and a thrill ran through me. I loved this fucking car. And even though she wasn't a fan, there was no way she could deny this thing was sexy as fuck. Maybe she'd be up for enacting another fantasy of fucking on the hood while the engine purred beneath her naked body.

The gravel of the parking lot crunched under the tires as the lights on the front of the bar shined through the partially snow obscured windows. A lone figure standing in the doorway in glittering shorts and a leather jacket had my pulse racing. Thankfully, I had left the mask on so no one would recognize me unless they were familiar with my car.

I knew I wasn't technically doing anything wrong, but since it was so out of character, I'd rather keep my newfound enthusiasm for masked role-playing a secret between me and the woman tied up and gagged in my back seat.

Not wanting to risk her rolling into the footwell, I carefully steered the car onto the main road that headed into town but turned in the opposite direction, heading up the winding part that led to the nearby mountains. From here on out, we were going to be all on our own.

It was still too early for there to be tourists in the rental cabins, because we were in that slow time of year where the summer and early fall hiking and rafting season had tapered off. Until the first solid snowfall, then they would return when ski season had officially started. The college kids tended to stay in town close to the university, and my family's land was too remote for the random passersby to see me carrying a woman with a gag and her hands zip tied into the cabin.

I just hoped my parents didn't see the front cameras activate and watch the footage. They were open-minded people—who I'd caught more than once with their own amorous activities—but since I still had the mask on, I didn't want them calling the cops. That would be an awkward conversation I wanted to avoid.

As I carefully navigated the turns, with my headlights the only illumination through the densely wooded forest, I periodically used the rearview mirror to keep an eye on my very willing, but naughty captive. Her face was tucked into the seat beside her, so I couldn't read her expression very well in the darkness, but it looked like she might have fallen asleep.

She had better get her rest now, because after getting a taste of what it was like to embrace this dark persona she'd requested, I craved more. She wanted me to act more like a bad boy, so I was going to be a very bad boy. At least in this part of our lives. Hopefully, she would be more understanding about the rest of my responsibilities if I salvaged this part of our relationship.

Maybe reconnecting—repeatedly—this weekend would be just what we needed to fix things.

The roads north of town were more densely covered with snow as the elevation rose. I'd already changed out the tires to prepare for winter, and I had a set of chains in the trunk, but it wasn't bad enough to need those yet. The snow glinting off the headlights gave the woods an ominous glow, but since it was bound to be freezing, I didn't plan to do any more chasing outside for the night.

I wanted to get the fire started, take her clothes off and forget the outside world while I lost myself in her body. My promise to bury my face between her legs was my first order of business, and then I'd bury something else there. A stray jealous thought distracted me as I considered she may have waxed her pussy with the intent to pick someone else to go home with tonight, but I hoped I was wrong because she hadn't hesitated since the moment I found her on the dance floor.

While it made it difficult to concentrate on the road, I plotted new ways to explore this more primal side of our sex life for the remainder of the drive. Just because we might be snowed in didn't mean we couldn't play.

There were plenty of places to hide in the cabin, and I wondered if she'd be up for an unclothed game of hide and go seek. Only when I found her, I'd fuck her. It seemed like a win-win for me.

"We're almost there." I announced, and her face rolled toward me, her eyes blinking sleepily in the dim lighting. There was something different that I couldn't place about her, but it might have just been because she was so agreeable for once. "Don't forget we're too far away for anyone to hear you, so trying to scream will just wear out your voice. I'd like to hear it screaming other things later, so I'm going to need you to be quiet."

She hummed, the sound muffled by the bandana I'd tied across her mouth, and I smiled, knowing she was still down for playing the game since she'd responded with a hum and not silence or a pissed off growl.

Slowing the car and carefully navigating it across the frozen gravel on our private driveway, I tried not to jostle her too much even though I was desperate to get her out of that back seat.

My cock was already hard, and I knew once she started leaning into her naughty role for the night that she'd make it even harder.

"If you even think about kicking me when I open this door—" I warned, eyeing the spikes on her heeled boots. "I'm gonna throw those fucking boots into the woods and we know you'd never make it far without shoes if you manage to escape. Although with this snow, I think you're trapped inside with me for the weekend. I'm sure I'll think of something we can do to pass the time."

When Mikey had told me to look for the pink boots, I'd admired how hot the thigh high black boots with pink soles made her legs look from across the dance floor. She'd looked so carefree as she let the music move her, and I couldn't recall a time when she'd looked so relaxed. Maybe this shift between us would bring back parts of the girl I'd initially been attracted to.

Once a college kid wearing a baseball uniform had started to make his move on where she danced with her arms stretched above her head and her hips swaying in a sensuous rhythm, I knew I needed to stake my claim and put my plan into motion. There was no way I was letting another man put his hands on her. Especially one who didn't deserve her.

"It's snowing pretty hard now, so I'm going to check the generator and get the fire started inside. I won't be long, but I need to know you'll be waiting for me when I get done. Can you be a good girl?"

Hooking my arm around my headrest, I looked in the back seat, watching her nod. I wanted to say fuck it and throw her over my shoulder now and get inside her the second we were in the cabin. But the ice crystals forming on my windshield had me more concerned for her safety. People died from exposure at this elevation in no time, and this weekend was all about pleasure, and only the fun kind of pain.

Watching her body language, I climbed out, the wind biting into my exposed skin since I'd given up my sweatshirt to her in the woods behind the bar. For once I was thankful for this annoying as fuck mask, because it'd protect my face. She remained still as I folded the seat forward, leaning into the car and grasping her hips to slide her across the seat.

She turned her head away from me, hiding her expression as she let me pull her out, only wobbling slightly in her heels when they hit the snow-covered gravel of the path leading to the house. Despite the black hoodie drowning her slight frame, she shivered, her lips quivering as her breath fogged around her red, puffy lips.

Lips that had thoroughly sucked my dick in a way they never had before, and I was desperate to get between them again.

But that could wait. We had days to play if this snow didn't let up. Anything over eight inches and we weren't going back down the mountain for days. But luckily, I had another eight inches to keep us distracted until then.

"Let's get you warmed up," I murmured, wrapping an arm around her back and leaning down to brace my other one behind her knees. She laid her head on my shoulder while I carried her toward the house, kicking snow out of the way.

She was quiet while I punched the code into the lock on the door and blinked curiously up at me as I nudged the door open. Using my elbow to press the switch, I expected the overhead lights to illuminate the front hallway, but nothing happened. Looked like my planning was for a good reason, because the electricity was out and wouldn't be coming back on tonight.

"Power's out. I'm gonna lay you on the couch. Can I take off the gag?"

She nodded, her lips curling around the cloth in her mouth in what I assumed was a smile.

Carefully laying her down on the worn cushions, I reached behind her, untying the cloth and pulling it free. She flexed her jaw and sighed, reaching her bound hands toward me. Her fingertips grazed the side of my mask like a caress, and I craved the feeling of them on my skin.

Reaching down again, I went to lift her mask, but her desperate plea stopped me. "No. Leave them on. Both of them. I'm not ready for this to be over yet."

Neither was I, but there was something almost panicked about the way she requested we remain anonymous for what happened next.

"Stay here. I'll be back in a few minutes. Anything you need before I go?" I knew I wasn't sticking to my menacing, masked persona, but it seemed she liked the combination of the character *and* me.

"Just come back to me."

Nodding, I left her there, somehow knowing she would stay where I placed her. She was just as anxious to connect as I was, and until we dropped back into character, she'd be patient.

Throwing on my Carhartt jacket hanging by the back door and a pair of work gloves from the shelf above the hook rail, I trudged through the accumulated snow and quickly brushed off the generator. It only took me a few minutes to get it purring to life, but

I only activated the portion that kept the appliances and the water heater running.

I was more concerned about our food supply and warm water than lights, and maybe spending the next few days in the dark would help keep the fantasy alive. There were plenty of battery-operated candles and lanterns if she wanted something more.

All I wanted was to lose myself in her for the foreseeable future until reality called us back.

Chapter Thirteen

Charley

As I stared at the wooden beams spanning the sloped ceiling of the cabin, memories of all the time I'd spent here in the last decade flooded in.

All the times I'd watched him from across the room, when he didn't even notice my curious eyes following his every move. Part of that desperate, lovesick schoolgirl was hidden deep inside of me, and I wanted to reassure her that everything would turn out alright after this weekend. That my heart would survive knowing this side of him.

Now that the rush of the chase and the raw sexual energy that pulsed between us in the bar had faded a bit, I was scared. Hudson wasn't just the object of an unrequited crush; he was my friend. And as desperate as I was to finally feel him inside me, I was terrified he'd reject me in the light of day.

I still had no idea if he'd connected the pieces that I wasn't his toxic monster of an ex, but he had to know things were different between us. It'd never felt like this with another man, and judging by the animalistic way his eyes had followed my every movement while I gave him head surrounded by the darkened forest, he'd never experienced something like that before either.

I couldn't exactly see Viv being an enthusiastic giver. Because the only thing she seemed to suck was the life out of people.

My heart raced as the back door slammed, making the cabin shake, followed by the sound of Hudson's feet stomping on the rug echoing down the hallway. The hum of the appliances kicking on subdued the silence, but every quiet footfall had me dreading his return.

"Don't worry," he chuckled from the other side of the large great room. "I'm not coming for you yet. Need to get the fire going so you're not cold when I strip that flimsy costume off you so I can keep you naked and begging for my cock until the snow stops."

I didn't respond, continuing to stare at the ceiling as I contemplated my next move. I was afraid to speak now that the adrenaline had worn off, for fear he'd recognize my voice. I knew we couldn't keep the masks on forever, and once they came off, I had no idea how he'd react.

There wouldn't be any hiding my identity or running away if we were going to be here until the storm cleared. I needed something to keep him distracted. Something to keep the game going until I could figure out what I'd say to him once my identity wasn't a secret anymore.

I shifted my legs, testing to see if the old pull-out couch would creak when I rolled myself onto the floor. It didn't, so I carefully propelled myself off the side, tucking my arms close to my chest so I didn't break something when I hit the plush rug covering the wood floor.

Shuffling to my knees, I watched Hudson hard at work stoking the fire, the muscles in his biceps flexing as he placed dry logs inside the stone fireplace. The hood of the mask still hung over the back of his head, and I felt a bit guilty that I'd convinced him to keep it on, because it couldn't be all that comfortable. The places where my mask was stuck to my face made my skin itch and it'd chafed where the elastic band stretched across my temples. But it was the only shield I had right now, and I wasn't going to take it off until I had to.

I awkwardly crawled on my knees to the edge of the rug, double checking that Hudson was distracted before I slowly crossed the distance to the kitchen. My bound hands slipped on the doorknob, but thankfully it opened without creaking. With the wall as leverage, I wobbled to my feet, using my shoulder to push the door almost closed.

This kitchen was where I'd spent countless hours, eating meals with the Rivera family or playing board games at the long rectangular table in the high back wooden chairs. I'd always been envious of Hudson and Hazel for having each other, despite the nearly six years of age between them. It was lonely being an only child even though I had cousins only a short drive to the neighboring town of Butterfly Ridge. My parents had been busy running the ranch when I was younger, so when Hudson's mother had taken me under her wing and included me in their trips to the cabin, I'd been thrilled.

It wasn't that I wanted to escape my family—my parents were great despite their hectic schedules—but when you grew up with horses as your closest friends, having a real family to spend time with was a welcome respite from loneliness.

"Already embracing your naughty role?" Hudson's voice echoed down the hallway, the hairs on my arms rising with the menacing tone he'd dropped back into.

Remaining quiet, I crouched and flattened myself against the wall next to the door, hoping it'd conceal my body if he opened it to look for me here. I wasn't sure what he'd do when he found me, but the idea of him punishing me was ratcheting up the arousal that built with every passing moment.

"You're just delaying the inevitable," his loud voice drifted from the other side of the cabin, and I had a feeling he'd already checked all three of the bedrooms to see if I'd hidden there. "When I find you, I'm going to bend you over my lap and turn that ass red."

While that declaration had me wanting to give my location away, I waited, knowing that there weren't that many other places for him to look.

The door swung slowly inward a few moments later, the shadow of its large frame concealing me in the darkness. He was quiet as he pulled open the cabinet doors, but the floor creaking beneath him made my pulse race because I knew eventually there would only be one remaining place to search.

"You think you're being sneaky, don't you?" he chuckled, his voice quieter than it'd been when he was in the hallway, which meant he knew I was in the kitchen with him.

Biting my bottom lip, I tried to remain quiet despite the burn in my legs from squatting in the high heeled boots I was wearing.

"I can smell you." His voice was a whisper as the door swung open, revealing my crouched position. The dark slats of his mask and tilt of his head should have looked ominous and threatening, but I knew this masked man only doled out pleasure. "And now I'm going to eat you."

"Aren't you going to punish me first?" I teased, biting down on my lip as I awaited his response.

"Hmmm, good point," he hummed, crouching down so we were at eye level. "But wouldn't it be a more effective punishment if I didn't spank you? Because I think you might enjoy it a little too much."

"Or you're worried about your skills."

His masked face suddenly loomed inches from me, indicating I'd hit my mark, a low growl emanating from his throat. "Guess we'd better find out."

"Bring it." I pressed myself tighter against the wall as he reached for me, screaming as he dragged me from my hiding place and pulled me upright against his chest.

"Don't worry. I'm not going to hurt you...*much.*" His dark chuckle against the side of my head as I thrashed against him almost made me laugh, but it turned into a moan as he forcibly turned me around and flattened me on top of the hardwood table.

The worn edge bit into the front of my thighs, his strong legs pinning me in place as his hand gripped the back of my neck. "Hold still or you're not going to like what I do."

"No," I hissed, bucking my hips into him.

"Fine. We'll play it your way," he growled, pulling the zip ties binding my wrists together above my head and hooking them around the spindle on the high back of the chair on the other side of the table. His bulky sweatshirt was next, Hudson wrenching it up my arms and throwing it forward, so it hung awkwardly off my bound wrists. "Now you have to stay put."

The position forced me onto the toes of my boots, the table just wide enough that it stretched me fully beneath him. I had to admire his quick thinking, because it'd keep me from getting any leverage if I struggled. If I pulled hard enough on the zip ties, I could probably get them to snap, but my arms would still be trapped, and the bite of the plastic into my wrists kept my adrenaline flowing.

"Hmm," he hummed, and I jumped as his facial hair scraped down the side of my neck, his full lips following. Either he'd taken the mask off, or pushed it out of the way, but he made no move to remove mine again. I cursed against the tabletop in front of me as his teeth scraped my sensitive skin, biting down on my nape as his large hands pushed my cropped top up.

"Fuck," I panted in a whimpery moan as his teeth sunk in further, his fingertips expertly pinching my nipples until they were hard.

"I think you like it when I touch you like this. Don't you? You want me to show how out of control you make me. How feral I've felt all night. So desperate to mark you so you know exactly who you belong to."

My heart pounded against the hard surface, tears pricking at the corners of my eyes at the thought of him really wanting that. Wanting *me* to belong to him.

"Answer me."

I hesitated and he leaned away, my body feeling cold as the warmth of him disappeared.

"Yes," I gasped as he reached beneath me, pulling at the button on my shorts. He wiggled them down, until I felt the bite of the cold air on my overheated skin.

"Fuck, this ass," he growled, his fingers digging into my exposed flesh hard enough he was bound to leave a mark. One I would slowly watch fade days from now wishing I could ink it onto my skin.

With hurried movements, he yanked the denim down my thighs, large hands bracing my calves as he pulled my shorts free. The cool surface of the table cooled the burn slightly, but as I heard the scrape of a chair on the wood floor behind me, I was suddenly on fire.

Fingertips traced between my legs, sliding in the moisture his filthy mouth had inspired and I whimpered, desperate for him to finally stop teasing me.

"Don't get shy on me now. I want to hear your moans. There's no one here to hear you scream but me. We're just getting started, my naughty girl."

Chapter Fourteen

"OH GOD," I MOANED as Hudson slowly pushed a finger inside, hooking it forward and pressing down while he pinned me in place with a firm hand on my lower back. It left me nowhere to go, and when his foot kicked my legs apart, I called out, the muscles in my thighs straining to keep me from falling.

"You look so fucking hot like this," he groaned, pressing his hips forward so I could feel how hard he was through his jeans. I wanted to scream for him to fuck me already, but when the pressure from my back disappeared and his large palm connected with the exposed skin of my ass, I suddenly wanted him to spank me more.

"Again," I groaned as he kneaded the skin roughly, the sting of his palm fading into something pleasurable.

"Fuck, I think you like this. You just got so wet." He added a second finger, slowly fucking me with them both as I wiggled my hips to get more friction. "You are a filthy, wet, desperate mess."

"More," I pleaded, almost frantic for him to do it again.

"Such a demanding little thing," he taunted, his palm smacking down again at a slightly different angle before he soothed away the sting. "And you mark so well for me. I can see your fair skin turning pink already."

"Make it redder."

"It's like you think you're in charge here." I could tell he was amused by my needy reaction, but I craved more. I wanted to feel the burn of his handprint rising on my flesh.

"More." I changed the tone of my voice to reflect the desperation I felt, and he obliged, the impact of his large palm making a smacking noise that was bordering on obscene.

"You're *so* fucking wet." His low voice matched my frantic need, and I whined as he withdrew his fingers. The sound of the chair scraping against the floor again had me shaking in anticipation, and a moan escaped when his hands pulled my ass cheeks apart, the tip of tongue sweeping between my legs. "And your taste...*fuck*."

The corner of my cheap plastic mask dug into my cheek as I collapsed against the table, completely at his mercy.

And the noises—the noises he made as he dove in had me shaking against the cool wood beneath my overheated body. When his fingers rejoined the mix, I screamed, clenching around them once I couldn't hold back any longer, my climax jolting me like an electric shock.

"Mmm, I think I love that sound," he chuckled, his wet lips dragging against the skin of my ass cheek before I felt the bite of his teeth against my tender skin. I cried out, but he didn't release me, his large hands holding my hips down while he traced his tongue along the indentions of his teeth marks. "And I fucking love seeing my marks on you."

My mouth was parched as I panted, trying to catch my breath while he continued to softly rub his nose and lips across my ass. It was definitely a new experience for me to have a guy nuzzling where he'd just left an imprint of his teeth on my ass cheek, but he seemed to be enjoying himself.

"Let's see what other noises we can get you to make," he chuckled in that low menacing tone. The chair clattered to the floor as he stood behind me, rustling for a moment before he smacked his hand onto the table beside my head.

I could barely make out the tiny square packet, surprised that after four years they still used condoms, but I guess I shouldn't have been. Viv didn't seem like the cream-pie type. But I wasn't going to let thoughts of her ruin this for us even if I was on birth control and wanted him to take me raw.

"Goddamn you're fucking hot." His deep groan almost drowned out the sound of his belt buckle, but the swish of the leather being wrenched from his belt loops made my eyes widen.

Would he really...?

"Fuck!" I shouted as the leather of his belt cracked down on the other side of my ass where he'd spanked and bitten me earlier.

"Louder," he growled, letting it smack against my skin a second time and I screamed, balling my fingers into tight fists in front of my face, the zip ties digging into my skin as I pulled against my restraints. "I'm gonna fuck you now, little devil. And the louder you are, the harder I'm gonna work to make you come again. If you stay quiet, I'm just going to fuck you until I come and leave you here, aching for me."

"Shit," I exhaled, trying to catch my breath and relish in the dull pain his marks had left behind. In my wildest fantasies, I never would have imagined Hudson to be the primal type, but I had a few toys I wanted to show him at my apartment that'd leave behind some lasting marks if he decided to touch me again after this was all over.

His palm slowly traced down the back of my thigh, slipping in between my legs and rubbing my clit softly until I was squirming again, still sensitive from my earlier orgasms.

"Mmm, so fucking wet." I could feel it coating my thighs, and the way his chest kept rumbling as he gently ran his hands along my overheated pussy had me getting even more excited. His fingertips paused at my entrance, slowly dipping inside before they retreated. Taunting me with their proximity.

Once he'd apparently had his fill of touching, his large, tattooed hand grasped the condom, the sound of it being ripped open mingling with his excited breaths.

A moan escaped me as his bare thighs pressed against the back of my legs, and I lamented that I wouldn't get to see his face when he pressed inside me for the first time. I wanted to watch his ridiculously long, dark eyelashes flutter as he filled me, see how his mouth dropped open as he slid in effortlessly, and watch the tendons in his neck flex when he bottomed out the first time.

But the sounds of it sent a thrill up my spine, enjoying the harsh grip his fingers had on either side of my waist. Reveling in the way my thighs shook as he pulled out for the first time before he rocked back in, pinning me to the wood beneath me.

"So good," he panted, his hand grasping the back of my shirt and twisting, using it as leverage to fuck me, his hips moving faster and harder with each thrust.

He pulled his fist back, the neckline of my top pressing into my throat as if it was his fingers. My lips and cheeks started to tingle as I gasped for air, but it just drove me closer to the edge. I'd almost forgotten that he wanted to hear me scream as I held my breath, pleasure licking up my spine as sweat broke out across my skin.

"Oh fuck. Harder," I moaned after a particularly hard thrust and he had the audacity to chuckle.

"What was that? I couldn't hear you."

"Harder!" I yelled, mindlessly tugging at the zip ties until my wrists burned. I knew it'd leave permanent marks if I didn't stop, but I couldn't. I didn't want to. I wanted the reminder. "Fuck me harder! Please! Oh, *fuck.* I'm so close."

"Gonna make this pussy come all over my cock," he groaned, increasing his pace until the table scraped across the floor with each thrust. The chair I was attached to rocked as it moved, banging against the wooden edge inches in front of my face as his hips brutally pressed me into the edge beneath my hips.

He leaned down, hot breaths fanning across the back of my neck as his arm shoved beneath my body, his fingers strumming my clit as he kept up his pace. My legs burned as the pleasure built, and I could hardly focus on anything except where we were joined. His body coaxed mine to follow his movements, moving as one as we both went barreling toward release.

"Come on, baby. Let go," he whispered into my hair, and I was gone, free falling into pleasure like I'd never felt before, the pain mingling with ecstasy and threatening to pull me under as I gasped for breath. "That'a girl. I can feel you. Squeeze that cock. I'm gonna come so hard now that you have."

His weight lifted off my back, my spent body collapsing onto the table, the sweat coating the surface beneath making my skin slide with each one of his thrusts. His feral grunts became louder as his fingers dug in deeper and I knew he'd be leaving more marks behind.

Relief flooded me as he cried out, sending curse words echoing against the walls of the kitchen. My eyes closed as my chest heaved, drawing in labored breaths. The blackness began to pull me under as I heard a snapping sound followed by my wrists being released from the harsh plastic that'd been keeping them captive.

Soft lips traced my skin, and tears pricked my eyes as his fingers traced over it, soothing away the ache.

"I'm sorry." His voice was a rough whisper as he gathered me into his arms, carrying me out of the kitchen and down the hallway while my body hung limply in his strong arms. "I didn't mean to get so carried away with you."

Cool sheets brushed against my skin before his fingers pulled my shirt over my head. He tugged on the edge of my mask, and I rolled away from him, curling onto my side.

"Let me take it off, baby," he whispered, slipping the elastic over my pigtails and rubbing his fingers over my sore temples. My scalp burned as he tugged my hair ties loose, combing his fingers through my chaotic waves.

His gentle touches briefly roused me from the euphoric stupor that'd overtaken my body, momentarily afraid he was going to roll me over and realize who I was. He simply pulled off my boots, throwing them onto the floor beside the bed. Quiet rustling was the only sound in the room, and then a large, warm body wrapped around me from behind, Hudson's lips resting against the back of my shoulder as he hugged me tightly to his chest. His large hands covered my bare breasts, and I hummed as he enveloped me in his warmth.

The last thing my exhausted brain registered was his soothing voice whispering words I couldn't decipher into my skin.

MY EYES BURNED AS my eyelashes fluttered, sunlight streaming around the edge of the curtain a few feet in front of my face.

Blinking hard, I tried to recall when my bed had gotten so close to the windows overlooking the back parking lot of the bar, but my heart raced when I focused on the wood paneling covering the wall next to this window.

I was in the cabin. At the Rivera's cabin in Hudson's bed—*naked*—while his hand possessively gripped my hip, and his warm breath fanned against my neck.

A filthy slideshow of the things we'd done together last night flashed behind my closed eyelids, and I felt my skin heat as I recalled all the things he'd done to my now weary body. I would blame it on alcohol, but I knew Hudson would never drive his baby after a drop of alcohol, and I hadn't drunk a thing before he found me on the dance floor.

My neck ached and the skin on my ass felt tender, Hudson's objective of marking me clearly achieved. Trying not to disturb the sleeping man behind me, I moved my wrists up, studying the deep indentations the zip ties had left behind. I wasn't sure how, but I hadn't broken the skin, although they'd probably visibly bruise.

As I cataloged where I felt the evidence of everything we'd done, my pulse raced when I realized I was more concerned about him freaking out because I was going to look bruised and bitten than I was of him being confronted with *me* lying in the bed next to him.

A soft snore escaped his mouth, and Hudson's large body shifted, rolling away from me. I knew I had to get out of this bed now before he rolled back and trapped me beneath his warm—strong, *nude*, tanned, tattooed, sexy body and...

Focus, Charley.

Moving carefully, I slowly inched my way down the mattress, careful not to pull the blankets with me as I slipped off the end.

The fronts of my thighs had purplish bruises from where they'd been pressed against the edge of the table, and I ran my fingertip over the mark, enjoying the brief flash of pain.

Hudson was sprawled across the bed on his side when I peeked over the edge, his nearly naked body stretched across the mattress, the corner of the quilt barely covering his legs. I tried not to let my gaze linger on the way his cock stretched across the sheets beside him, proving morning wood was not a myth.

Most of my hookups over the years hadn't spent the night, and I wasn't really a fan of repeats. Feelings were messy, and now I was going to have to deal with mine.

Best case scenario, Hudson would freak out and I'd be able to talk him down. Maybe he'd realize how perfect we were for each other, and he'd fuck my brains out again.

Worst case scenario, Hudson would freak out and never talk to me again, kicking me out into the snow to find my way back to civilization or die somewhere alone in the woods.

Reality would probably fall somewhere in the middle, but I wanted to avoid reality for as long as possible.

My knees ached from where they were scratched as I crawled naked across the cold wood floor of his bedroom. I slipped into the dark bathroom and prayed that there would be enough warm water to wash away the dread clinging to my skin.

Chapter Fifteen

THE SOUND OF RUNNING water lingered somewhere in my subconscious as I stretched against the sheets beneath me, reaching across the mattress for her warm body. My fingers were met with cold cotton, the only proof that I went to bed wrapped around a beautiful woman was the scent of her lingering on the pillow beside my face. She must have gotten a new shampoo, and the scent just made me hungrier to lose myself in her soft, curvy body again.

Blinking, my blind search was confirmed when I opened my eyes to empty sheets next to me, a sliver of bright light streaming around the edge of the curtains and illuminating the dim room. The sound of the generator hummed outside, and I shifted across the mattress to pull open the curtains.

White stretched as far as my eyes could see, snow covered tree trunks sprouting out from the fresh untouched powder. There had to be at least a foot covering the ground, if not more, and I was thankful I'd had the foresight to stock the cabin in case we couldn't leave. Because the last time we got a foot up here, I had to dig the gravel driveway out by hand once we knew the main road had been cleared.

It was early for this much snow, so the county wouldn't necessarily have the best response with plowing. Especially when I know I saw most of the plow drivers at the bar last night tying one on. I doubted they'd be too motivated to get around to plowing this far up the mountain until tomorrow...or maybe even the next day.

They tried to get all the streets in town cleared before they headed up the treacherous mountain pass.

The knowledge we'd be trapped here for days with limited electricity had filthy scenarios wandering through my brain, imagining all the ways I could use her body to bring us both pleasure.

Her submission to my lead had been completely unexpected, and it was freeing to let all the fleeting intrusive thoughts I'd previously had during sex take the wheel. This whole role-play situation may not have been my idea initially, but I was embracing the sense of freedom that had blossomed inside me.

The way our bodies moved together, and how she responded to me was completely different than before. I was afraid that in the light of day, the changes between us would fade away and we would be right back where we were a few days ago. Not knowing where to move forward from this.

Phenomenally dirty sex wasn't going to solve the problems, but hopefully, it'd show the path forward.

The pipes squealed as the water turned off, gentle feminine humming carrying through the mostly closed door. I smiled at the sound, knowing that my performance last night might be the cause of her good mood.

Rising from the bed, I padded across the cold wooden floor and rested my hand against the door. I didn't want to disturb her morning routine, but I also wasn't sure if she knew to look under the sink for the emergency lantern, so she wouldn't have to be in there in the dark.

After listening to her happily hum for a few more moments, the sudden need to touch her overcame me, and I pushed lightly, the door slowly creaking open.

"Shit!" she shrieked, my hand immediately meeting resistance as she pushed back against me.

"Are you alright?" I chuckled, wanting her to let me in so I could wrap her in my arms and drag her back to bed with me.

"Fine! I'm fine!" she yelled; her voice pitched high. The door clicked shut and the sound of the lock engaging made me laugh.

"You don't need to lock me out, I've seen it all before." My comment was met with silence, so I continued on. "And I'd like to see it again. Don't bother getting dressed, I don't want anything getting in my way."

After no response, I sat down on the edge of the bed, bracing my forearms on my thighs as I waited for her to come out.

"Did you fall in?" I yelled, expecting her to charge through the door with her hands on her hips, but that was not what happened.

The lock disengaged and the door slowly swung open. It was nearly pitch-black inside, but I could see the shadowy outline of the lantern on the counter.

She stood there in the shadows, her face not visible, but the thin strip of light from the window showed her nervously shifting her legs together.

"Everything okay?"

The hair on the back of my neck stood up when she didn't respond, and I almost expected her to lunge at me like this was the beginning of a bad zombie apocalypse movie.

"I didn't hurt you, did I?" I whispered, recalling how rough I'd been with her once we'd gotten to the cabin.

"No." Her voice was a soft, but there was something about it that had me sitting up straighter and pulling the corner of the blanket over my lap.

Before she even took one step, I knew my life was going to be forever changed from this moment forward.

"It looks worse than it is."

Guilt crashed through me as she took a step into the sliver of light, pinkish red scratches winding up her shins and skating across her knees. Another step and her wrists were visible, angry marks marring her skin.

I was so busy cataloging each new mark that I was caught off guard when her face came into view.

"Holy fuck!" I shouted, scooting away from her, up the mattress, pulling the comforter across my crotch. It would have been understandable for my morning wood to wither at the sight of my little sister's best friend standing there in nothing but a worn T-shirt, but it taunted me beneath the material while I was freaking the fuck out. "What the fuck are you doing here? Did you and Hazel follow us up here last night? Why are you in my bathroom?"

She paused, her mouth hanging open, my traitorous cock practically waving at her from beneath the covers. This was bad. This was so fucking bad.

"I think you know who brought me up here," she said quietly, but my eyes still widened at the way the corner of her mouth turned up. I'd seen that smirk aimed at me countless times across a worn bar top, but never while she was only wearing my shirt, covered in bruises that I'd left on her skin in a moment of passion so intense I was afraid I imagined it.

"Why aren't you wearing more clothes?" I yelled, knowing that her flimsy costume was currently in a pile on the floor next to my bed and on the floor in the kitchen where I'd...

"Because your shirt was the easiest thing for me to grab."

"Go find some fucking clothes, Char! For fuck's sake. Don't just stand there half naked!"

Her chest shook as she watched me scramble to pull the blankets to cover more of my naked body. I tried not to ogle her, but she looked so sensuous standing there with her hair down in chaotic blonde waves, tipped with teal dye.

"I thought your hair was fucking purple?"

She bent over at the waist as she let out a laugh, and I slapped my hand over my eyes when I got an eyeful of her naked tits through the neckline of my V-neck shirt.

"Go!" I shouted, pointing blindly in the direction of the door. "Go find something to cover that up. You're practically fucking naked. Fuck!"

"I don't have anything but my costume to wear," she responded, her voice calm, but I could tell she was entertained by my panic.

"Hazel has shit in her room. Hell, go find something of mom's and put it on. The more skin covered, the better."

"Like you said," she teased. "You've seen all of it before."

"For fuck's sake, Charley. Now is not the time to make jokes. Just go. I'll meet you in the kitchen."

Once I've appropriately freaked the fuck out.

I pulled down my hand and watched her scurry out the door, my shirt riding high on the backs of her thighs, a bruise in the shape of my teeth peeking out the bottom. It took all my self-control not to follow her. Not to pin her to the wall and demand answers. But I couldn't be in the same fucking room with her right now.

Once I heard the door down the hallway close, I yanked off the covers, my fingers flexing as I tried to ignore the problem that hadn't abated below my waist.

I should have been worried that I'd clearly just fucked my little sister's best friend and then spent the night wrapped around her naked body because of Vivienne, but honestly that wasn't why I was so thrown.

And I should have felt guilty, but I didn't. Because when it came down to it, I'd gone to that party as a single man. And I'd pursued a beautiful woman. A beautiful woman I probably should have never laid my hands on. But now that I had...

I wasn't sure if I could ever look at her the same way again. And I wasn't sure I wanted to.

Charley had been in my life off and on for over a decade. She was my little sister's best friend. I shouldn't know what she looked like with her lips wrapped around my cock.

I shouldn't know what the sexy whimpers that she couldn't hold back while her pussy was milking my fingers sounded like. I shouldn't know what it felt like to have her tits in my hands and her hard nipples between my fingers and pressing against my tongue.

I shouldn't know what it felt like to slide into her body and know that it'd never *ever* once felt that good to be inside a woman.

And I sure as fuck shouldn't know that there was a deep, hungry, primal part of myself that wanted to do it all again.

My cock flexed as I walked into the bathroom, and I glared at the traitorous appendage. "This is your fault."

The emergency lantern cast ominous shadows across the small room, the mirror still covered in the condensation that had built up while Charley had been in the shower. Naked. Wet. Running her fingers over the marks I'd left on her body because I'd craved seeing a fleeting reminder of what it felt like to touch her last night like some craved the high of a drug.

"Fucking hell," I cursed as I used my palm to clear the mirror, staring into my face.

While my mind felt overwhelmed, my face looked relaxed, the bags that were usually dark underneath my eyes softened and my eyes looking brighter than I'd seen them in months.

Running my hand through my chaotic hair, I tried to resist the urge to turn. But I failed, taking in the long scratches that covered my lower back from her nails. And I also failed to block out the way it'd felt to have her hands on me, to have her lips on me—just as hungry for me as I was for her.

That kind of animalistic attraction was rare, and if I was completely honest with myself. I'd never felt it before...not until last night.

Even when I'd pulled her against me on the dance floor, I felt the electric spark, and it'd just built exponentially with every touch until I'd filled the condom—I'd thankfully put on last night—with my cum.

It wasn't that I didn't trust Charley, but the last thing I needed right now was to accidentally kidnap my sister's best friend and then get her pregnant.

Even though I wanted to turn the water on hot enough to scald my skin, I settled for a more tepid temperature, knowing that I needed to conserve the amount of electricity the hot water heater used from the generator.

Closing my eyes under the spray of the water, unbidden images of last night flashed through my mind. And the more that I recalled, the more I realized I should have known from the start that it was Charley I was touching.

Maybe some hidden part of myself had known and done it anyway. Maybe the attraction that I'd denied to Reid was real. Maybe I'd been unknowingly watching her for months, wanting to touch her. Maybe this attraction had started the first time I heard the creak of the bed that'd once been mine in the room above my office. And maybe I'd burned with jealousy when I heard some other man coaxing moans out of her.

Knowing I had to finish up and go face Charley, who I was going to be trapped with for the next few days, I washed my body quickly, avoiding the part of myself that was throbbing.

But the lure was too great, and I stroked myself with a desperation I couldn't control. And when I came, it was to the thought that before we left, I wanted to come inside her again, I wanted it to be bare, and I wanted to look into her eyes when it happened—knowing it was her.

Guilt consumed me as I dried myself, only growing as I pulled open the drawers of my dresser, cursing when I realized I hadn't replaced the clothes in it since I was in high school. After rifling through the drawers, I realized there wasn't anything that'd fit me except for a pair of flannel pajama pants.

Knowing I'd stalled long enough, I grabbed the rumpled clothing off the floor beside my bed, and made my way to the laundry room, tossing Charley's clothing into the washer. I passed Hazel's bedroom on the way down the hallway, searching for my shirt on the floor, but I had a feeling Charley was still wearing it.

My suspicion was confirmed when I paused at the open kitchen door, watching her turn a pancake over on the griddle covering the gas stovetop. A full pot of coffee sat on the counter beside her with two mugs, and she already had a covered plate full of what smelled like bacon.

"Do you want chocolate chips?" she asked, not looking in my direction. I wondered if she felt the same sensation whenever I was near that I'd noticed over the last few months.

"I didn't buy any," I replied, leaning against the doorframe to watch her work.

She turned in my direction, flashing me a teasing wink. "I know where the secret stash is kept."

Her eyes drifted to my bare chest, lingering in a way that I knew would turn me on if she wasn't careful. "I thought we needed to cover up. Walking around shirtless, clearly not wearing underwear doesn't seem like accomplishing that goal, Hudson."

"The only T-shirts in my drawers are too tight. And I wasn't exactly in the mood for an ugly sweater." I was avoiding the missing underwear, because I'd wrenched it off after I'd tugged it on, deciding if she didn't need to wear any, neither did I.

"We both know you would have put it on if you were so determined to hide from me."

Changing the subject before I needed to hide something else from her, I crossed my arms over my chest.

"You didn't have to cook for me." And now I felt guilty that I hadn't thought to feed her. It was the least I could do after what I put her through last night. But I hadn't slept that hard in years.

"We both need to eat. Seemed selfish to only make myself something. And I wanted to." She averted her eyes back to the pancakes, but there was no disguising the blush on her cheeks.

"I'm sorry." My voice was low, but I knew she heard me when her body stiffened, her hands dropping to grip the edge of the counter.

"You don't have anything to be sorry for."

In the bright sunlight streaming through the windows facing the woods behind the cabin, I scanned her body, each new visible mark adding to my guilt. "I hurt you."

Charley ignored my comment as she transferred the pancakes to a plate, turned off the burner, slammed the spatula against the counter and turned toward me with a glare.

"Let's get this out of the way now. I'm the one who should be apologizing for what happened. And I don't regret a single mark you left on me last night. So, you need to quit freaking out about this because I don't want to spend the entire weekend with you apologizing to me when you didn't do anything wrong."

"Fuck. Of course I'm freaking out Char, I assaulted my little sister's best friend."

She reached for the plates perched on the corner of the kitchen table and my eyes widened as I noticed the condom wrapper and the broken zip ties lying in the middle of the table.

Reaching past her to grab the incriminating evidence, I balled it inside my fist, the plastic biting into my palm like it must have bitten into the fragile skin of her wrists.

She laid her hand on my bare shoulder, her touch scalding me. "Hudson. Stop. You did not assault me."

"But I did. I thought you were…" My voice cut off abruptly, and I lowered my voice, turning in her direction. "But you weren't, and I never asked for consent or…"

"Do you honestly think I would've run into the woods behind the bar and let just anyone chase me?" she asked, her fingers lingering on my skin before she pulled her hand away.

"But you didn't know it was me. And now Hazel is going to think someone kidnapped you and call the police. Then they're going to arrest me and…"

"Take a fucking breath, Hudson. Hazel knows I'm with you. I texted her last night when you went back into the bar. I saw the mask in the backpack on your desk when I dropped off my tips. I knew it was you from the beginning. And it's not like the tattoos on your hands wouldn't have been a dead giveaway."

"You knew it was me?" A part of me was relieved, that she hadn't been that naive to put herself into a potentially dangerous situation like that. But the other part of me was floored. Why hadn't she said anything?

"Duh. That's what I just said. Keep up." Her teasing grin shouldn't have made my pulse race, but it did.

"And you didn't stop me?"

She sighed as she stared down at the table, her chest rising and falling underneath my shirt before she looked back up again.

"No, at first I was a little startled, but I was also really turned on when you started whispering in my ear."

Arousal flooded my system, my mind immediately going to a fantasy where I grasped her waist and propped her up on the table we'd already defiled, stripping every last piece of clothing off her…

"I turned you on?" That was the part that was throwing me off. While I'd had fleeting inappropriate thoughts about her, I never imagined she would be experiencing the same thing.

"Wasn't the first time. And hopefully won't be the last."

"Wait, what? I've turned you on before? When?"

"You're gonna need to get me a notepad. It's kind of a long list," she teased, turning around and plating the food she'd made. She extended a plate in my direction like she'd just told me the weather and not that last night wasn't the first time I'd turned her on.

I just stood there dumbfounded, refusing to fully face her because I knew the unruly appendage in my pants would give me away. "What?"

"Take this, and let's go sit down." Her eyes lingered on the chair I'd had her fucking zip tied to last night, my cock twitching at the memory. "On one of the couches. I don't think my ass would like me if I sat in one of those."

When I didn't move, she laughed, pushing the edge of my plate into my chest. "Come on."

Her shoulder brushed my chest as she stepped around me to walk through the door, and I suddenly had the urge to throw myself into the snow outside the back door. Because I was so hard I was afraid that my cock would never go down.

Chapter Sixteen

M Y HANDS SHOOK WITH nerves as I carried my breakfast out to the great room, placing it on the table in front of the fireplace. I seriously needed to take a seat before I spilled coffee all over myself.

Holy shit.

I knew this morning would change things, but I hadn't expected to feel so fucking anxious in Hudson's presence. And thrown off by the heat in his eyes after I confessed that last night wasn't the first time he'd turned me on. He had to know how attractive he was. Women hit on him all the time. But he was so fucking loyal I doubted he'd looked at another woman in four years.

Before I could freak out again, feeling a misplaced sense of guilt toward Viv of all fucking people, Hudson sat down on the couch beside me.

"Were you serious in there?" he asked, leaning back into the corner of the couch. He casually brought his mug to his lips, taking a sip. When I didn't answer him, he raised an eyebrow, and I fought the urge to crawl into his lap.

The man was like catnip, and my pussy was feeling particularly feral this morning.

Deciding that maybe it was better just to get my feelings out in the open, I let all the thoughts that I'd kept inside for a long time out in one nervous ramble.

"You're really fucking hot. And you used to spend half the summer with your shirt off. But that isn't why you turn me on. You're a catch. Like I can't believe how much of a catch you are sometimes because of all the dumb shit you and Reid did in high school. But the post college glow up on your personality—despite your *horrible* taste in girlfriends—was pretty fucking unexpected. I tried to hate you. I *wanted* to hate you, but you made it really fucking difficult. Did you honestly not realize I had a crush on you?"

"No."

"Men." His deep chuckle after I rolled my eyes made me feel warm inside.

And now he was staring at me with a stunned expression on his really fucking hot face that caused me to unleash a stream of verbal diarrhea I couldn't take back.

"You really have no idea how kind you are. Like looking at you, you'd expect some cocky, tattooed asshole who thought his shit didn't stink, but you're not. You're humble, and you admit when you're wrong. You always try to see the best in people—or at least that's the only fucking reason I can come up with as to why you let that emotional vampire of a woman yank you around for four years."

"She wasn't that bad in the beginning..." he said quietly, but the glare I gave him in response had him shutting his mouth.

"Yes, she was. You never saw the nasty side of her personality that she only aimed at Hazel and me. But I'll forgive a mistake you made when you were twenty-six driven by hormones. Just like I'm hoping you'll forgive me for not telling you who I was last night while we were on the dance floor. I should have said something, but I didn't."

Hudson turned, placing his coffee on the table, and bracing his forearms on his thighs.

My fingers itched with the need to touch him, but I just watched as he processed everything I'd just said to him.

It was...a lot.

"How long?"

If I wasn't paying attention to his every move, I might have missed the whispered question. I'd been embarrassingly honest with him up to this point, but confessing how long he'd been the benchmark I judged every other man by brought out the nervous sarcasm.

"Well, from what I remember of last night, it was a pretty solid seven, maybe even an eight, but you might need to let me check again."

"Not my dick, holy fucking shit, Charley," he growled. "How long have you had a crush on me?"

"I met you when I was ten." He froze, slowly turning his head in my direction, and I suddenly wanted to take my chances surviving in the snow outside when I saw the panicked expression on his face.

"Oh my God. I'm a fucking pervert. I slept with..." he whispered, but I cut him off before the panic spiral could start.

"Hudson, I'm twenty-five. I'm not a preteen girl with a childish fascination anymore." He nodded, but his hands were still balled into fists. "I'm also not going to apologize for liking you. You now know I think you're pretty fucking amazing. And now that Viv is out of the picture..."

He looked stricken when I finally said her name.

"I thought you were her."

Nodding, I bit my lip and whispered the question that had been building in my head since last night. "But did you really?"

"I, uh..." he stuttered, but I knew my hunch was right, and I pushed on.

"You guys have been together for over four years. Did it ever feel like that with her?"

He scrubbed his hands over his face before he shook his head. "I thought maybe it was the adrenaline or something."

"Yeah, or *something*. Your ex was a self-centered bitch who was never nice to you. And you knew the moment you shoved your hand into my shorts that I was not her. You probably knew before that while I had my lips wrapped around your dick."

"I..." he trailed off, but judging by the deep exhale he let out, he was coming to the same realization I had. He knew deep down that he was with someone else, but once he got that first rush of the chase, he kept going.

"I'm willing to bet she never got down on her knees like that for you either."

"That's... is that really any of your business?"

"No, but the fact you're not denying it is enough of a confirmation for me. You knew it wasn't her before you fucked me. And you did it anyway."

And I wasn't going to let him talk himself out of enjoying it. He craved the rush of sex that intense like I did.

"And I'm willing to bet she never would have let you mark her like this." I grabbed his hand, pulling it toward me and placing it on the bruise covering my upper thigh.

His thumb traced the marred skin, and I knew his sister was never getting these shorts back. Because his gentle touch was making me ruin them since I still wasn't wearing any underwear.

Using my other hand, I turned his face toward me. His eyes followed my fingers as I gently pulled down the neckline of his shirt, showing him the bite mark on my neck.

He reached out, tracing his fingertip over the bruise forming.

"Last night was... I've never done anything like that before. I'm sorry if I hurt you."

"You don't need to be sorry. It's not that big of a deal."

He shook his head, wrapping his warm palm around the back of my neck and bringing his forehead to touch mine.

"It is to me. I don't ever want to hurt you."

Closing my eyes and breathing him in for a moment, I lowered my voice and reassured him that everything was okay between us. Or at least I hoped it would be. "Hudson, I was practically begging you to do it. It's okay that we got a little carried away when we fucked. If I wanted to stop you, I would have."

"You *should* have."

"Because you think I shouldn't want you?"

He shook his head, his warm breath coasting across my lips. He was so close, but I didn't dare move for fear he'd pull away from me completely.

"Because I want you." His fingers tightened on the back of my neck, his thumb tracing the tender skin on the side of my neck where he'd marked me. "And I don't think I can stop. Not knowing what I do now."

My heart pounded as he held me there. And I hoped he'd let himself feel the intensity of the connection between us.

"Then don't fucking stop."

Chapter
Seventeen

"Please stop cursing, Charley," I begged, my face shifting to the side, our noses brushing against each other.

"Why? Does it make you hard when I say *fucking*?" she teased, her voice barely a whisper.

She had no idea. My head had been a chaotic mess since she told me that she knew how to fuck while she was leaning across my desk yesterday. It had unlocked a hidden part of myself that I hadn't realized was there. A part that saw her as more than just my little sister's best friend.

My fingers twitched and I had to force myself not to press harder. She had no idea how much I was struggling with my attraction to her. Now that the box had been opened...

"Give me a break here, Char."

She had the audacity to giggle, and I had to tamp down the physical urge I had to haul her into my lap and do naughty, depraved things to her now that I knew how much she liked it.

We needed to talk. And there would be no talking if she stayed this close to me for much longer.

"Are you really mad, Hud?" The corner of my mouth quirked with her the abbreviated version of my name that she knew I hated. "You going to *spank* me?"

All the blood in the rest of my body rushed to my unruly cock, and I dug my fingers into the sides of her neck. My primal, horny inner demon clawed its way out of the recesses of my mind where I'd shoved him last night when I wrapped my arms around her soft, naked body before we drifted off into the most peaceful sleep I'd had in years.

"Actually yes," I growled. "Get over here."

That damn giggle returned, and she leaned forward, our lips centimeters from brushing together. She licked her lips, the tip of her tongue sweeping across mine.

Loosening my grip on her neck, I leaned in, expecting my lips to finally capture hers. But that wasn't what happened.

She ducked, sliding off the couch and crawling across the rug before she pushed to her feet.

"You have to catch me first."

A rumbling groan built in my chest. This girl wanted me to chase her with the biggest hard on of my life, when seconds ago I thought we were finally going to kiss.

A kiss that I never expected to want so much, but I now fiercely craved.

I wanted to tug on her pouty lower lip with my teeth, bruise her lips, pin her to a wall and devour her mouth…

"Shit." When my eyes refocused, she was gone. But from my hunt for her last night in a cabin I'd spent half my life in, I knew there were only so many places to hide. Taking a minute to calm myself down, I breathed in through my nose, slowly letting it out of my mouth. This little temptress was going to give me high blood pressure at thirty years old.

Charley was barefoot, wearing only my T-shirt and a pair of tiny athletic shorts. Surely, she wasn't crazy enough to run out into the snow, but when I heard the back door slam, my eyes widened. I ran down the hallway, cursing when I saw a pair of boots missing and a sizable pile of snow on the rug that led from the hallway into the mudroom to the open back door. When I was close enough to see past the doorway, I noticed deep indentations tracked through the snow outside the door, leading around the corner of the house.

"You're going to fucking freeze out there!" I yelled, yanking my coat off the hook and zipping it up so it covered my bare chest. I shoved my feet into a pair of boots and took off after her.

"Then I guess you better catch me!" she yelled back, but she didn't sound that far away as I stepped out into the snow.

"You're fucking crazy, Charley!"

Her devious giggles were the only thing I could hear as I made my way through the foot of snow, turning the corner in just enough time to see her slip around the next corner of the house, her blonde hair at least covered by one of my knit hats. An oversized black coat drowned her slight form. *My* coat.

At least she wasn't totally reckless because I really would be punishing her for running out into the snow with barely anything covering her. If she gave herself frostbite, I couldn't continue doing all the nasty things I wanted to do to her.

When I turned the corner to follow her tracks heading back toward the front porch, I didn't have time to react before a handful of wet snow was flung into my face.

"You're in fucking trouble now," I growled, picking up the pace in enough time to grab her around the waist as she stepped onto the concrete front step.

"I hope so!" she laughed, thrashing in the tight hold I had on her.

"You're gonna hit me in the damn junk," I groaned as she landed a kick with her snow boots to my shin. Maybe it was payback for how rough I was on her last night, and she wanted to leave some more marks of her own.

She stopped struggling, looking back at me over her shoulder. "Well, we don't want that. I have plans."

I couldn't hold in the laugh, depositing her back onto the ground and spinning her around to face me. She jumped and I grasped the back of her thighs while she wrapped her bare legs around my waist.

"It's gonna be fucking frozen at this rate."

She cupped my cheek as I backed her up against the wooden front door, pressing her against it, a sick thrill running through me as her eyes widened when she realized how cold it was. "Then maybe we need to do something to warm it up."

"You'd like that, wouldn't you?"

"I am a bit partial to the idea, yeah. But I didn't get a very good look at it in the dark last night. I wasn't kidding when I said I needed to get a better look. Might not be as impressive as I thought it was."

Narrowing my eyes, I pressed her harder against the door, my chest rumbling. "Didn't stop it from choking you last night or keep you from coming all over it once I finally got inside that tight, wet, bare pussy."

Her eyes widened, a grin pulling at her lips. "You're filthier than I thought you'd be."

"I could say the same."

"You thought about me?" she asked, suddenly looking vulnerable.

Deciding to be honest with her—be honest with myself. "Every fucking time I heard your headboard thump against the wall when I was trying to concentrate on payroll or supply orders. I wanted to be the one making you moan like that. Even if it wasn't right."

"Nothing's stopping you now," she whispered, leaning in closer.

Our foggy breath mingled in the space between us, her gaze softer than I expected. She was right. There wasn't any reason we couldn't have this. At this moment. Right now. We could embrace this insane, probably incendiary, attraction and just let this weekend play out naturally.

"I don't want you to regret this once you aren't trapped here with me."

"Hudson," she murmured, leaning forward until her lips brushed mine. "I could never regret you. Even if this all blows up in my face."

"I thought you liked that part," I teased, barely brushing my lips across hers in the whisper of a kiss.

"I do. So much..."

I couldn't tell you which one of us closed the distance first, but soon we were both gasping against each other's lips in between ravenous kisses. Her teeth tugged on my lip in a way that had my cock throbbing inside my flimsy pajama pants despite the frigid temperatures.

"Why did we wait so long to do this?" she asked, panting as I trailed biting kisses down her neck.

"Because I'm a fucking dumbass," I growled, stepping back and hurriedly punching the code into the door lock. It was a harsh reality that I'd wasted so much time with the wrong woman, but I wasn't wasting any more.

She yanked down the zipper on my coat, scraping her nails down my chest as I stepped inside, slamming the door and pinning her against the back of it.

"Naked," she groaned as I sucked on her collarbone, leaving another faint mark on her delicate skin beneath the one I'd left last night while I'd been inside her. "I want you naked."

"Fuck," I groaned, leaning away from her to pull down the zipper on the old coat of mine that covered her. We both peeled it off her shoulders, letting it drop to the ground with the one I'd been wearing at our feet.

She gasped as my cold fingers crept underneath the T-shirt, pushing it up. Her tits looked even better when I could actually see them, and I hadn't been kidding when I told her I wanted to fuck them. But right now, I wanted to fuck *her* more.

Diving in once the shirt had been thrown somewhere behind me, I nipped and sucked at her skin. Her fingers pulled my hair, and I groaned as she alternated between trying to pull it out at the roots and using the leverage to shove my face into her chest.

"Quit fucking testing me," I growled, pulling her hand away from me and pressing it against the door above her head while I balanced her weight with my other arm.

"But it's so much fun...*Hud*. And why are you allowed to curse and I'm not? I'm not a child, as you've clearly noticed. I can use bad words too."

Oh, now she wanted to talk about this. She was the one who'd gotten me all riled up by making me chase her around the house in the cold fucking snow. And now she wanted to talk.

"This is all some colossal joke to you, isn't it?"

She tried to hold in a giggle but failed, and I growled, making her eyes light up.

"You are driving me literally fucking insane. Do you want me to fuck you right now or do you want to talk about why it makes me want to spank you every time I hear a curse word come out of those pouty fucking lips?"

She bit down on the corner of her lip, shrugging. I literally had her pinned to the front door with her amazing fucking tits in my face and she wasn't letting me enjoy my time with them. Now that I could see them in the light of day, I wanted to dive in and never come up for air.

"You really want me to spank you again, don't you?"

She nodded, a wicked gleam in her eyes. The little devil knew that by delaying my gratification she'd be riling me up. Making me desperate for her.

"Took you that long to figure it out, *Daddy*?"

Her breathy whisper should not have made me even harder, but she was not calling me that. I felt guilty enough that I was taking advantage of someone who was five and a half years younger than me. I'd rather she be screaming out my real name.

"Don't call me that. The only name coming out of your mouth better fucking be mine."

She shook her head, rocking her hips forward in a way that made my eyes cross. All that was keeping me from ramming into her was a pair of flimsy shorts and a thin layer of flannel.

"Why do you keep making things so hard?"

"Hmm," she hummed, rocking against me again. "Feels pretty hard right now."

"Charley." I growled. Knowing that what I was about to do was reckless. "Stop me if you don't want this. One word and I stop."

She nodded, so I continued.

"Are you on birth control?" Her eyes widened, but I knew it wasn't because she was scared when a wicked grin pulled at her kiss swollen lips.

"Yes."

One quiet whisper was all it took for my control to snap, and I crushed my lips to hers as I yanked at my pajama pants, freeing my weeping cock.

She moaned as I pulled at her shorts, growling when I realized I'd have to put her down to get them off her. Lowering her to her feet, I spun her toward the door, pressing her palms against the wood before I yanked at the waistband of her shorts, a sick thrill running through me as the material ripped. I let the destroyed shorts fall down her legs, grabbing a handful of her ass as I pressed my chest against her back.

"I've never fucked anyone raw before," I whispered into her ear before I leaned down, rubbing the tip of my nose over her bite mark, enjoying the way she shuddered against me.

"Neither have I," she breathed, pressing her ass back into my crotch.

"I want to watch my cum run down your thighs after we're done."

"Oh God." Charley arched against me, and I used the opportunity to grasp her breasts in my hands, roughly pinching her nipples before one of my hands explored lower.

"I want to fuck you bare for the next two days and know that I'm the only one who's ever had you that way. Is that what you want from me?"

"Yes," she gasped, pulling one of her hands from the door and digging her nails into the front of my thigh. "Do it."

Shifting my hips back, I guided myself between her legs, groaning against the back of her neck when I felt how wet she was. This was probably a terrible idea, but I trusted her, and I didn't have the self-control to stop.

"Fuck," I exhaled into her hair as I pushed inside, her breathy moan activating the part of my brain I hadn't known existed before her.

My hands grasped her hips tight enough I knew I'd leave more marks as I drew away and thrust back inside hard, watching as her fingers grasped at the wooden door in desperation.

"You drive me fucking wild, Char. I've never felt as out of control as I do when I'm inside you."

"Same," she gasped, pressing back into each of my brutal thrusts.

Using my boots to kick hers wider, I bent my knees and thrust into her in desperation to connect with her in a way I hadn't with anyone before.

Tucking my face into her neck, I wrapped an arm around her, grasping one of her tits in my hand, slowly tracing my other hand down the smooth skin of her stomach and to where we were joined.

The noise she made when I grazed her clit had me clenching my jaw, resisting the urge to sink my teeth into her soft skin.

"Fuck," I groaned, clenching my eyes when she started bucking into each one of my thrusts, chasing the release I desperately wanted to give her. "I wanna feel you come on me so fucking much."

She let out a gaspy moan, arching against me, her legs shaking as she finally let go, squeezing my cock as she came hard.

Knowing how rough she liked it, I pulled back, grasping her waist with one hand to anchor her as I brought my other palm down against her ass.

She screamed when I did it again, and I watched with sick fascination as each strike left a red imprint of my palm on her fair skin.

When her forehead thumped against the door in front of her, her back arching and a flush covering the skin on her neck as she let go again, I couldn't hold back anymore. Using her hips as leverage, I fucked her brutally, using her to drive myself right over the edge, pulsing inside her shaking body.

My chest was heaving as I wrapped my arms around her, holding her to me as we both tried to catch our breath. She seemed to be just as desperate for my touch, reaching back and holding my sweaty head against her, scratching her fingernails against my scalp.

"I don't think I'm ever going to get enough of you," I whispered into her hair, finally letting the feelings I'd been trying to hold back flow through me.

I'd tried to convince myself that I shouldn't be feeling what I was because of who she was. But I couldn't deny that she was one of my favorite people. All the talks we'd had closing the bar together drifted through my head as I clutched her to me.

She was my friend, she was always the first one to jump in to help without strings attached, and maybe it was the time the lens of her being only my little sister's best friend was shattered.

She would always be important to Hazel. But she could be something else for me.

She could be my future.

Chapter
Eighteen

Charley

I SHOULD HAVE BEEN a little squicked out by the fact that I currently had cum stuck to my thighs while I wore a pair of baggy flannel pajama pants four sizes too big. I should have...but I wasn't.

Sitting on the plush rug across from Hudson at the coffee table next to the fireplace, a thrill ran through me every time I laughed and felt the evidence of our intense coupling leaking out of my now sore lady parts.

Playing mindless board games and talking was the most I'd ever seen him smile since I'd known him. And I craved each and every one of them.

When we were outside the stress of the bar, he was lighter, more talkative, and he looked at me in a way that made my entire body light up. For as much as he'd been horrified when I walked out of his bathroom this morning, he was making up for it with his inability to go more than a few minutes without touching me in some way.

Subtle finger grazes gave me goosebumps, his hand settling on my calf underneath the table made me desperate to climb across it, and it took everything in me not to swoon when he kissed my neck before he escaped to the kitchen to grab more snacks.

Vivienne was a fucking moron. Like really fucking stupid. Because she had this man who, despite his tendencies to be a workaholic, went out of his way to make her feel special. To show her genuine affection. I knew it wasn't his idea to go to every stupid local festival he went to with her where he held her hand and carried her things the entire time.

I knew he wasn't perfect. I wasn't blind to the fact that he could withdraw into himself and never asked for help. His responses most afternoons before the bar opened often consisted of a litany of grumpy grunts and growls. He was oblivious to things sometimes—like the fact that women hit on him constantly when he was behind the bar. But he tried. He gave a shit. He listened to what people said and was kind in a way I knew was rare.

He was a solid guy. And so eager to please. But in a 'make my nasty fantasies come to life' kind of way, not in the 'too sensitive or gentle way.' But if that's what I wanted, I knew he'd do that too.

Now that I'd seen this more primal side of him, it worried me that if he suddenly decided he wanted to stop whatever was happening between us, I'd be crushed. If I thought it was hard to want him before, it would be impossible if he walked away.

I'd have to quit the bar, find somewhere else to live and escape to Butterfly Ridge early to work for my aunt and uncle while I finished my degree. Commuting twenty minutes would be the least of my worries.

"You okay?" he asked, flexing his fingers, and shuffling the UNO cards he held.

Nodding, I tried to push down my nerves. Because he was here with me now. He insisted we stay dressed for the rest of the day and talk instead of getting distracted by each other's bodies. That meant he cared what I had to say, not only what I looked like naked and writhing across whatever surface he'd spread me across.

I was currently drowning in fabric, zipped inside his black hoodie with his T-shirt underneath. He'd pulled his pajama pants on me after removing our snow boots, then proceeded down the hallway naked with both pairs in his hands to return to the mud room before he went to find more clothes.

He hadn't been kidding about things not fitting him when I'd teased him about being shirtless earlier—not that I'd minded that much.

A Sage Springs football T-shirt was currently having its seams brutally tested as it hugged his defined chest, and his long legs were covered with another pair of soft flannel pants.

"Yeah, just thinking."

"Do I dare ask about what?" he teased with a knowing smile. While he surely expected me to be thinking about something dirty as I often was, I was dwelling on the fact this man held my heart in his large, calloused hands.

"I'm trying to figure out how we can play strip UNO," I teased, and he rolled his eyes.

"Why do you keep testing me like this? We're behaving right now."

"Because it's fun." He returned my cheesy grin, and I knew he wasn't really annoyed with me. "And I think you need that right now."

"What? Someone to drive me insane?" All the teasing was pushing his boundaries, but I think he was starting to crave the way I pushed him. I know I craved the effect he'd had on me.

"No, fun. I don't think you've let yourself have fun in years. And maybe I'm tired of letting you hide behind a failed relationship with someone who never appreciated what she had."

He swallowed hard, placing the cards down on the table as he stared at me. "She…"

"Was fun until she realized she couldn't turn the sweet man she thought was a bad boy into her lapdog."

Smack talking other women wasn't something I wanted to do. But after every snide comment she'd made behind his back for the last four years, I was tired of being nice about it for the sake of my friend. She wasn't nice to him, and if I had to remind him how terrible she was, then I'd do it until he finally stopped trying to romanticize the memory of her to make himself feel guilty for doing what he wanted for once.

"I'm not that sweet," he murmured, his previous smile gone. A pang of remorse flowed through me, but she was always going to be the elephant in the room until we addressed it. I knew it'd only been days since they broke up, but I wasn't going to be a rebound fuck if I had anything to say about it.

"Yeah. *You are*. But you've also shown me that there's a darker side you've been burying because you knew little miss perfect would never be okay with it." And I craved it. Every mark. Every degrading word. Every time he let himself lose control.

"She was the one who wanted me to…" he trailed off, looking down at the table and avoiding eye contact.

"Put on a mask and chase her through the woods?"

"Yeah…"

Taking a breath, I let him know exactly what I thought about how this situation started, and how it would have ended if he had tried it with her. "And she would've been into it once, critiqued your performance—which was really fucking hot, by the way—and then strung you along until the next time you weren't giving her enough attention."

He nodded, clenching his jaw as he tapped the edge of the card deck against the table.

"I'm not going to tell you she was terrible a hundred percent of the time. And I know that you…" I hesitated, choking out the next word. "…loved her. But she was honest with you last week and showed you who she was and how much she valued you. Don't let her take up space in your heart when it's clear she doesn't want you in hers."

His eyes flashed toward mine briefly before he looked down again. "She wanted to date other people and make me wait around for her to *decide if what we had was worth coming back to.*"

Growling, it almost morphed into a laugh at the way the corner of his mouth turned up in amusement at my defensive nature.

"Down girl," he teased, exhaling and shuffling the cards one more time.

"Know your worth, Hudson. You deserve more than someone who wants to string you along until she's bored with her next victim."

"And you deserve more than the string of one-night stands you take back to your apartment to torture me."

"Maybe that was my plan all along," I giggled, rubbing my toes against his thigh underneath the table.

"Wouldn't surprise me," he laughed, tossing a stack of brightly colored cards at me from across the table. "Maybe once you beat me, I'll let you UNO reverse cowgirl me."

I giggled, picking up my cards and fanning them out to plan my method of attack. I'd reverse cowgirl that bucking bronco any day of the week.

THE FIREPLACE CRACKLED BEHIND me, casting an ominous glow across the dimly lit great room. I should have been asleep, but after I'd awoken in the dark, my heart beating frantically as I tried not to dwell on the panic of my dream, I knew it'd be futile to try to go back to sleep.

Hudson had been out cold. In his defense, once we'd finally succumbed to the tension that'd been building all day, we'd frantically had sex three times—in varying acrobatic positions and unconventional locations—until we'd fallen asleep long after midnight.

Then my subconscious had decided to be a bitch, and I had a nightmare about a manic vampire dressed Harley Quinn chasing me through the woods intent to stab me to death and drain all my blood. It didn't take a genius to figure out that the vampire was more of the emotional kind, and I was worried that maybe I'd kicked the hornet's nest when I'd brought up Viv yesterday.

Hudson hadn't seemed upset with me, per se, afterward, but he had been uncharacteristically quiet while we cooked dinner together last night. I was trying not to read into it too much. He'd had a rough week, but I was determined to make it clear that I was here for him, and not just as a warm body.

But this morning, he was going to be my warm body to command.

Stretching my legs out in front of me on the coffee table, I tried to pull the hem of his hoodie down a bit further so my bare legs—and other parts—didn't stick to the heavily lacquered wooden surface.

"God this thing is terrible," I grumbled, scratching at the edge of my jaw, where the hard plastic of the mask he'd been wearing rubbed against my skin. It'd looked sexy and intimidating in the dim lighting of the dance floor during the party, and the dark of the woods behind the bar, but I was worried Hudson would stumble out here half awake and decide I was ridiculous for doing this.

He'd taken control during every interaction so far, but it was my turn.

And there was a huge difference between me taking the lead in the bedroom because we'd both like it, and me demanding control because I wasn't willing to satisfy anyone's needs but my own. This was for his enjoyment just as much as mine.

But Hudson had better fucking wake up soon, because now I was starting to second guess my sleep deprived plan to flip the script on him. Except for the chasing part. Cause the temperature had dropped outside overnight and it was too fucking cold to chase him through the woods when there weren't any warm clothes in the house that actually fit me.

"Charley?" Hudson's sleepy voice carried down the hallway, and I nervously shifted, trying to look like I had control of the situation. I could fake it until I made it with the best of them.

Deciding to stay in the role, I silently remained where I was, stretched across the table in only his sweatshirt, his mask and my knee-high leather boots.

"What are you doing up so early?" he asked as he appeared at the end of the hallway. His long arms stretched above his head as he yawned with his eyes closed. One more step into the great room and he'd see me.

And judging by the tenting in the front of his worn blue pajama pants, he seemed to be *up* for a little fun this morning. *I fucking loved morning wood.*

His footsteps halted the moment I came into view, the flames from the fireplace reflected in his wide eyes. "Holy fuck."

"Such a mouth on you," I teased, beckoning him to come closer with my finger.

"Never fucking said I didn't," he laughed. "Clearly, someone is feeling naughty this morning."

"Hmm. Have you been a naughty boy, Hudson?"

He took another step toward me, and I held up my hand, indicating for him to stop.

"Are you wearing anything underneath that sweatshirt?" he asked in a low voice, his eyes shifting down to where I had my legs crossed.

"No," I chuckled, keeping my voice low.

"Show me," he ordered, trying to take a step forward, but I shook my head, pointing my finger at him.

"You're not the one giving orders this morning, Mr. Rivera."

"And you are?" he asked, taking a defiant step forward.

"If you want to have a warm body to put your cock inside instead of your lonely, cold hand, then yes. I am fucking in charge."

He growled at my cursing, his cock flexing behind the material of his flannel pants. I pushed down the intrusive thoughts that wanted to say fuck it and pull him forward, rip down those pants and swallow him whole.

"But I think you want something a little bit more accommodating. Something tight," I whispered, uncrossing my legs and bringing my knees together. "Warm... *Wet...*"

"Fuck," he grunted, pressing his hand against his now fully hard cock.

"Take off the pants," I ordered, letting my knees fall open, revealing my bare pussy to his hungry eyes.

"You really are a little devil," he murmured, pulling the elastic waistband away from his waist and carefully freeing himself before he pushed them to the floor.

"Right now, I'm *your* devil. And you'll keep doing what I tell you to."

"Oh," he growled, wrapping his palm around his cock and squeezing while I watched him roughly stroke himself. "I'd like to see you be the one who takes control."

"Then you're in luck. Get on your knees, Hudson."

His eyes locked on mine, holding me captive as he slowly lowered himself to the carpet on his knees. He arched an eyebrow, daring me to continue to boss him around. But there wasn't any turning back now.

"Lean forward." I waited until he braced himself on his palms, his biceps flexing and making the ink on his arms undulate. "Now crawl."

He licked his lips, looking down to stare at where my legs were still propped open with a hungry look on his face. Good. Then we had the same objective this morning.

Him making good on his dirty promise in the woods to bury his face in my bare pussy.

When he was only a few feet away, I held my hand up for him to stop, and scooted off the end of the table.

"Back to your knees."

He shifted to sit back on his heels, his hands braced on his thighs, flexing against the skin, clearly trying to fight the urge to take back control.

It was so fucking hot that he was doing this for me. And when I told him so, a growl rumbled in his chest.

"Such a good boy," I murmured, stepping forward and placing a finger underneath his chin to force him to look up at me. He stared into my eyes for a moment, and then slowly exhaled, clearly finding something in mine that helped him relax. "So eager to please."

"You know I only want to bring you pleasure," he murmured, wrapping a palm around the back of my thigh.

"Hands off," I barked, moving back slightly. Bracing my hand on his shoulder, I lifted my boot to press the heel into the tattoo covering his pec, adrenaline racing through my veins as he groaned, and his cock flexed between his legs. Maybe Hudson liked a little bit of pain too. "I don't need your hands right now."

"My hands aren't the part that wants to fuck you," he growled, reaching for me again.

I dragged the boot up his chest, pivoting the toe over his shoulder and digging the heel into his collarbone. He groaned as I leaned down, panting when I grasped the hair on the side of his head.

"The only part of you that is going to fuck me right now is that wicked tongue. Maybe if you can't talk, you'll listen to my directions."

His eyes widened, but I could tell my harsh words were welcomed by the fire inside them.

"Lay down, hands at your sides." He obeyed, shifting to sit on his ass, holding my boot to his shoulder and pressing it into himself before releasing me, laying back against the carpet.

The hungry part of me wanted to say fuck it—literally—and sit down on the hard protrusion bobbing in the air between his thighs, but that would be giving him what he wanted. Right now, I was *taking* what I wanted.

Throwing a leg over his waist to stand over his body, my boot grazing his hard cock, I loomed over him. His hands balled into tight fists, and I watched as he resisted the urge to pull me down. His eyes briefly darted to where I knew he could see up his hoodie, but he just clenched his jaw, not saying a word.

Knowing I had his full attention, I unzipped the hoodie, peeling it off my body and throwing it in the direction of the coffee table. Deciding to tease him a little, I grasped my breasts, squeezing them before I pinched my nipples, moaning.

A rumbling hum built in his chest, but he didn't say a word as I lowered myself to my knees, sitting on his chest with his biceps trapped between my thighs.

"You're going to make me come—*without* the use of your hands. And when you do, I'll fuck you until you make me come again. If you don't listen to my directions, I'll leave you like this, desperate for me. If you're a good boy, I'll let you come inside me. And when I stand up, you're going to lick it off my thighs."

He flexed his jaw, a growl forming in the chest that heaved underneath me, brushing against my thighs with each heavy inhalation, but he didn't say no.

"Are you ready to show me what you can do with this?" I asked, leaning forward to cup his jaw, rubbing my thumb along his bottom lip before I pressed it inside his mouth. When he bit down, sending a flash of pain through me that had me squirming, I had my confirmation that he was fully on board with what would happen next.

Chapter Nineteen

Hudson

I T WAS TAKING EVERY single fucking ounce of self-control not to flip her backward, spread her out on the carpet, rip that fucking mask right off her face, and fuck her until she screamed.

But I was going to be a good boy, and I was going to do what she said. And if she accidentally suffocated me while she sat on my face, I was going out buried in my happy place. Because there wasn't anyone else on the planet that I would trust to let myself play like this with.

Charley wasn't just adventurous in bed, she let me embrace the intrusive thoughts I'd silenced for years, and I was determined to do the same for her. I wanted to be the person she felt comfortable enough to explore with. I wanted her to trust me like I trusted her.

"You ready?" she asked, petting the side of my face with her other hand as I rubbed the tip of my tongue over her thumb, nipping at it again like I was desperate to nip at her clit the same way.

Nodding, I took a deep breath when she shifted back to her knees, straddling my face. I could smell how excited she was, my cock bobbing as my tongue darted out and flicked teasingly against her clit.

She moaned and grasped my hair, rocking down into my face, hovering while I licked, sucked, and thrust my tongue into her wet, warm pussy.

It was difficult to resist the urge to grasp her hips and pull her down, and even more difficult to resist the urge to stroke my cock as beads of precum rolled down the length while she whimpered and rode my tongue. But the longer she drew this out, the harder I knew I'd come later, when I was buried inside her again. I'd become addicted to taking her bare and I was never going back.

"Mmm," I hummed against her, enjoying the way her hips dropped, and she ground against my lips, moaning when my teeth grazed her clit.

She wasn't shy about using me for her pleasure, and when her moans took on a high-pitched note—despite being muffled by the cheap plastic of my mask—I knew she was teetering on the edge.

Latching onto her clit with my lips, I drew it into my mouth and frantically rubbed the tip of my tongue against it, growling when she tried to escape the overwhelming sensations. My short fingernails dug into my palms as I tried to resist the urge to hold her in place, waiting until she rocked forward again to suck hard, repeating the same combination until she was screaming and shaking, pinching her own nipples while I watched her fall apart above me.

"Holy, fucking..." she panted as she sat back, giving me space to breathe despite the weight of her hips on my chest.

"Facing you or reverse?" she asked, licking her lips. "I'll let you choose."

"UNO reverse," I growled, aching as I waited for her to shift back, bracing her hands on my thighs as she rose enough to turn herself around.

"Oh, fuck," she whimpered as she lowered herself, taking the tip of my throbbing erection into her warm body, her pussy still clenching with the aftereffects of her previous release. "You're so fucking hard."

Relaxing and slowly lowering her hips until I was buried as deep as I could be inside her. I bit my lip to keep from groaning in satisfaction. It'd never been this good before. And not just because she was the only woman I'd ever let fuck me without anything between us. But because it was her. And in less than forty-eight hours, I'd become helplessly addicted to her—and I didn't mean just her pussy. Although that was pretty spectacular, too.

"Grab my hair," she panted, her voice muffled inside the mask. Rocking her hips slowly back and forth—she rode me, fire racing up my spine as I sat up, bracing myself with my other hand fisting the carpet beneath. I gathered her long hair at the base of her neck beneath the hood, and twisted it around my wrist, tight enough she had to arch backward, her movements becoming more frantic as she chased her second release.

"So good," I panted, unable to keep quiet any longer. "You feel so fucking good."

"Harder," she moaned, rocking frantically, digging her fingernails into my thighs as I began to thrust up from beneath her. "Fuck me harder. Make me come."

My thighs burned as I pushed into her, my forearm flexing as I fought to keep a firm grip on her hair.

"Oh God, oh God," she moaned, collapsing backward into my chest as she came, squeezing me inside her until my eyes crossed.

Unable to hold on any longer, I came, my cock jolting inside of her, setting off another set of moans while I filled her quivering pussy.

"I can't breathe," she panted, and I immediately released my hold on her hair. Reaching for the mask, I ripped it off and threw it to the side.

Holding her to me with one arm while I balanced myself with the other, I coached her to breathe with me.

"In," I whispered, flattening my palm over her heart. "Out."

She gasped for air, shaking as she came down, her tired muscles giving out as she collapsed onto my body.

"I've got you." Her breathing evened out and she relaxed into my chest.

"That thing makes it impossible to breathe," she whispered once she'd fully relaxed against me after her breathing evened out. "I don't know how you kept that thing on so long."

"Not gonna lie, it kinda sucked. But it was worth it since I got to end the night buried inside you."

Despite the release we'd shared a few minutes ago, desperation to possess her pleasure had me reacting as she shifted in my lap. I traced my hands down her sides, my right one drifting in between her legs. She was making a mess of herself as my cum leaked out of her, and I had a command—that I was suddenly more desperate than I'd expected—to obey.

"Stand up, Char," I whispered, holding her waist as she climbed to her feet. Pulling her backward, I leaned in, licking a line up the back of her legs, sinking my teeth lightly into her ass. She yelped and I pressed a hand into her lower back. "Bend forward."

She exhaled hard when my tongue slipped between her thighs, tracing up the inside of one until my nose was buried in her wet pussy. She squirmed as I lapped at her, cleaning her up like she'd wanted until she was moaning and leaning back into my movements. I hooked an arm around her thigh, strumming her clit softly with my thumb until she was shaking and calling out my name, throbbing against my lips.

"Mmm," I hummed, placing a kiss on her ass.

She turned and ran one hand through my chaotic hair, cupping my jaw with the other and tracing her thumb across my bottom lip. "I didn't think you'd actually do it."

"Get down here and kiss me," I murmured, and she climbed into my lap, her tongue hungrily sucking mine as she rocked against my cock that was throbbing for her.

"You're hard again," she whispered against my lips, reaching between us and stroking it in her fist while I moaned into her mouth. "I thought you older men were supposed to take a while to recover."

"It's your fault," I groaned, flexing my hips into her fist with each downward stroke.

She leaned back, sitting between my open thighs and spreading her legs. She gave me one final rough stroke and then grabbed my hand, bringing it to my now throbbing erection. "Your turn. Give me a show."

"I've got a better idea," I growled, laying her back against the rug. I swiped my cock through the wetness between her legs, dipping inside and then pulling it free—glistening with both of our earlier releases.

Climbing over her, I guided her hands to her breasts. "Hold these for me."

Her eyes lit up as I leaned down, biting her nipples and then alternating sucking them into my mouth until she was moaning and squirming.

Deciding to just go for it, I spit in the valley between her breasts a few times, spreading it around with my fingertips before I scooted forward, angling my dick to press in between them.

She watched with wide eyes as I slowly rocked, groaning as the combination of our cum and my spit had me gliding against her smooth skin. Seeing her reaction had me on edge in minutes, and I was clenching my teeth trying to hold onto some dignity. "If you don't want me to cover you in cum, tell me now."

And I swear to the fucking devil themself, she opened her mouth and stuck out her tongue. If I wasn't convinced this girl was meant for me after the last two days, I was now. And I would never let her go.

She moaned along with me as my balls drew up, cum splattering her chest. Stream after stream arched out of me, leaving filthy streaks across her neck and cheek. Once I was done, she reached forward, grasping the back of my thigh and pulling me forward to lick the tip, a tortured groan escaping my lips as she sucked me clean.

"That was hot. I give it an eight," she teased, wiping her cheek with her pointer finger and sucking it between her lips.

"Only eight?" I panted, smiling down at her.

"Yeah, eight points for the eight inches. Or should I go find a ruler to verify before I score you?"

"Ruining the moment here, Charley," I growled, scooting back to stretch my body over hers, our warm, sweaty chests brushing together. Wiping her soiled cheek with my thumb, I pressed it to her lips, watching as she licked it clean. "But I love how filthy you are. Lying here covered in my cum."

"And I *love...*" she paused, biting down on the pad of my thumb and wrapping her arms and legs around my suddenly fatigued body. "Being covered by you."

It was way too soon to have the feelings that I knew were coursing through my veins, and I would not be letting them out because I was worried that she wouldn't take them seriously at this point. But it went deeper than fascination. I was falling for her in a matter of days. Maybe I'd been under her spell longer than I'd realized, and once I was free of the toxicity that'd been plaguing me, my eyes had finally been opened to how amazing she was and how free I felt when I was with her.

"I like being surrounded by you too." She held me tighter, kissing me until I could barely breathe. "But you're getting kind of clingy."

She laughed, tucking her face into my neck, and I rolled to my side, pulling her into my chest and twirling her hair around my finger until we both drifted off to sleep.

Chapter Twenty

Hudson

S UNDAY PASSED MUCH THE same as Saturday. We spent the day talking about anything and everything—playing several games of twenty questions, getting progressively dirtier as the day went along. By the afternoon we were desperate for each other again, falling into bed exhausted and sore. We ate sandwiches in bed at midnight after we woke up again and then talked until the sun came up.

By the time Monday morning rolled around, my anxiety had started taking over, knowing our time living together inside these four walls was fleeting. The snow had tapered off and the temperature had risen, the sun shining brightly outside.

Part of me wanted to completely ignore the thawing snow, staying here long after it melted off and ignoring the world outside. But when I pulled my phone off the charger after I'd made Charley breakfast and left her to shower by herself, the screen was full of text notifications.

> *Hazel: Are you two ever coming up for air? Mom is about to send Dad up there to dig you two out. She's worried that Charley will never come to Christmas this year if she's stuck there with you for too long.*

As if I intended to give Charley another option. She was now welcome at all the family events she'd been welcome at before this, but for a whole new reason.

> *Hazel: I didn't tell her you were probably doing gross things to her furniture.*

Laughing, I responded, ignoring her digging for information that little sisters shouldn't know about their brother's sex lives. If she and Charley were really as close as they appeared, she likely knew this confinement was not platonic.

Hudson: She's fine. And I'll drag her up here if she tries to back out of it. White elephant stockings is a tradition, and she's not missing it.

Hazel: Does that mean that you two...

Hudson: It means that I really like your friend.

Hazel: And...

Hudson: And I don't want to let her out of my sight long enough to get sick of me.

Hazel: Sounds counterintuitive. But maybe the Stockholm Syndrome has finally set in.

Hudson: She's here because she wants to be, not because I accidentally kidnapped her.

Hazel: Mmhmm, sure.

She sent a GIF of a woman nodding and mouthing the same words.

Hudson: She's mine now.

Hazel: She'll always love me more.

Not if I had anything to say about it.

Hazel: The county has been plowing for the last two days straight. They're hitting the pass today. The bar is fine. Annie made sure everyone made it in for their shifts.

Fuck. That meant our hours were dwindling.

Closing out of the thread with Hazel, I clicked on one from Reid's cousin Jayden who lived in Butterfly Ridge.

Jayden: Reid told me you were stranded.

Jayden: Just cleared the pass. You should be able to dig out now.

Jayden: Let me know if you want me to come back and help, I can switch out my blade.

Hudson: Thanks man, I think we're good, but I'll let you know.

Jayden: We? Reid told me you were up there with Hazel's bestie.

Hudson: I am. Long story. We've been stranded since Friday night.

Jayden: Want me to push the snow back into place?

I laughed, kind of wishing he hadn't been able to make it up here. But with the weather clearing, I knew we'd need to get back to open the bar. Annie, my head bartender, would continue to cover like she had for the last few days if I needed her to, but I knew Charley and I were both on the next shift together.

"Everything okay?" Charley asked, sitting down on my lap sideways and wrapping her arms around my neck.

"Yeah. Road is clear."

"Oh," she whispered, her eyes scanning my face. I think she could tell I wasn't thrilled about the development, but we couldn't keep living up here and ignoring the rest of the world. At least not until my next stretch of uninterrupted days off.

"I'll need to dig out the gravel part of the driveway by hand."

She nodded, running her fingers through my hair and scratching my scalp in the way she'd realized made me want to purr like a cat and rub up against her. One of the perks of not being able to keep our hands off each other for three days straight was knowing what touches the other craved.

"I'll help if you find me pants."

Squeezing her thigh, I rubbed the damp skin, smoothing my palm over her knee. "I kinda like you without pants."

"And I kinda like not having a frozen vagina. So, find me something warm to wear and I'll help you."

"That eager to get out of here and away from me?"

"No," she shook her head, leaning down to kiss my lips softly, lingering briefly. "But if I help you then you won't be too tired to fuck me before we have to go back into town."

"So dirty," I whispered, tugging on the ends of her damp hair.

"I'd like to think of it as filthily well endowed. Like someone else I know who has a very *creative* vocabulary."

Shaking my head, I rose from the couch, pulling her into my arms. She laid her head on my shoulder as I carried her down the hall, sitting her down on the bench in the mud room. I crossed the room and pulled out all the cold weather work gear from the wooden trunk in the corner and started sorting through it for something that might fit her.

Once I'd found what I was looking for, I returned to where she was quietly watching me, pulling my old, insulated base layer, followed by a pair of thick, waterproof canvas pants up her legs, and cinching the waist belt so it was snug around her waist. I wrapped the black coat she'd worn before around her, zipping it up until the collar covered her chin.

She was drowning in my old gear as I pulled on a thick pair of wool socks and the snow boots that'd fit her before. A thick knit cap covered her blonde hair, and I carefully tucked it inside the collar.

"I am capable of dressing myself, you know," she teased with a muffled voice, her eyes full of mirth through the narrow space surrounding her eyes as she watched me pull on my gear across the room.

"Don't be a brat, Charley. You wanted to help and I kind of like your parts not frostbitten."

"But I'm so good at being one," she laughed, pulling on the pair of gloves I'd tossed in her direction.

"That you are," I agreed, pulling on my hat and grabbing the metal industrial snow shovels from the closet in the corner.

"I bet this thing can do some damage," she commented, teasingly lifting it and pretending it was too heavy for her to carry.

Deciding to lean into this new me who didn't bury his intrusive thoughts, I grasped her hand and held it to my heavily covered crotch. "I know this can."

"Yeah, tell me about it," she scoffed, rolling her eyes. "I'm gonna walk funny for days."

"Not sorry," I laughed, leaning in to kiss her temple before I opened the back door.

The cold wind bit at my exposed cheeks, and I wanted to slam the door and lock it, but I followed Charley out into the snow, to clear the path to our way home.

T HE SUN WAS HIGH in the sky by the time we finished, the remaining snow on the driveway melting off as we cleared the snow off my car.

For the first time ever, I prayed for the Chevelle not to start, but the engine purred to life on the first try. Charley's defeated expression as she sat in the passenger seat surely matched mine as I turned it back off and pulled out the key.

"We can stay here."

Her voice was quiet as she covered my hand, squeezing it briefly. "No, we can't. But I wish we could too."

"Fuck," I sighed, reaching over to cup the back of her neck. She hummed against my lips as I kissed her, my panic at the thought of leaving making me desperate to touch her now. "Inside or I'm fucking you in this car."

"I'd much prefer *on* this car. But it's a little too cold right now for that."

"We're coming back to that later once it's warm outside," I promised, opening the door and heading toward the house. She followed, and by the time we'd made it to the bedroom, we were both naked and desperate to reconnect.

But as I came inside her for the last time during our seclusion, I wasn't as scared as I thought I'd be. She seemed just as eager to be with me, never allowing more than an inch of space between our bodies.

"We need to pack," I whispered into her sweaty neck, softly kissing the bruised bite mark that'd started to yellow around the edges sometime in the last day. The horny demon hoped she wouldn't cover it up tonight. Because I wanted everyone to know she was mine. Maybe I could have Reid tattoo *Property of Hudson* across her cleavage instead of her ass.

She nodded, reluctantly untangling our limbs before she sat on the edge of the bed beside me, pulling on her borrowed clothing.

"We're going to have a talk about your lack of panties."

She looked over her shoulder at me with a smile. "I'm behind on laundry."

"I may have a washer you can fill with your load," I teased, pulling her backward and wrapping my naked body around her clothed one with my face tucked in her neck.

"Pretty sure *I'm* the one that gets filled with *your* load."

"That's during the spin cycle. My machine is off balance."

She giggled as I let her go. "And I'm the one with the dirty mind."

Standing from the bed to gather the clothes I'd been wearing at the party, I got dressed and extended my hand toward her. "Want to wear the snow boots back? You can leave them in my car, and I'll bring them back with me next time I come up."

She held her knee-high boots in front of the pair of flannel pants she was wearing. "You don't think they match? The website said they go with any outfit."

"Come on," I reached for her hand, lacing my fingers with hers. "It's time to go home."

I wanted to ask her to come to my house instead of me taking her to the apartment, but I knew we both had things we needed to take care of.

Charley was quiet as she followed me to the car, her hand clasped in one hand while I held the cooler with leftover food in the other since the power still hadn't been restored.

Not knowing what to say, we remained silent on the ride down the mountain, my hand resting on the soft cotton covering her thigh and wishing I could touch her bare skin. I craved the connection, but I knew this couldn't be the last time I'd have her in this car with my hand in the same place. Touching her like this felt as natural as breathing. Just like everything else where she was concerned.

When I parked the car near the freshly plowed back entrance of the bar, my fingers tightened, her smaller hand covering mine as she turned toward me.

"I don't want you to go," I whispered, leaning in to softly ghost my lips across hers.

"I don't either, but we can't sit in this car for the rest of our lives." She sounded sad, and I felt the same way, but I wasn't sure what to say right now.

"I'll be back once I dig out my driveway and take a shower."

She nodded, hesitating before she gathered her things and reached for the door handle.

I wanted to beg her to stay, or for her to let me come upstairs with her—suddenly terrified if I let her out of my sight that something bad would happen—but we both knew I needed to go home.

She stepped out of the car, and I watched through the frosted glass of the windshield as she unlocked the back door, turning to wave before she stepped inside and let the door close behind her.

I stared at the back door for longer than I should have, willing her to come back out before someone standing beside the car startled me.

Chapter
Twenty-One

Hudson

"**W**HAT THE FUCK, DUDE?" Reid's loud voice startled me as he pounded on my passenger window.

His grin was obnoxious as I rolled down the window, and I knew Hazel must have told him that my seclusion with Charley wasn't just platonic.

"Get in," I sighed, motioning to the passenger seat. He could help me dig out the driveway. It was the least he could do after he subjected all the patrons of my bar to his nipple accessories.

"You fucked Charley," he blurted out before he'd even closed the door. "Atta boy."

"Shut up and buckle your seat belt. You're helping me shovel my driveway and then I'm taking a hot shower before I indulge in your need for gossip."

"I already shoveled it." Of course he did, the helpful fucker. He made it hard to be annoyed with him. But it wasn't his fault I was grumpy this morning.

"Thanks."

"And I pitched that god awful Joker costume—I'm assuming Viv left on your porch—into the dumpster at the shop."

"The what?" There hadn't been anything on my porch before I left for the bar on Friday.

"There was a garment bag from the costume shop in Butterfly Ridge sitting on your front door mat covered in a foot of snow. The jacket inside was trashed by the time I found it, so I threw it away."

"She's gonna lose her shit," I groaned, wishing I could just forget the last four years. Now that I'd spent uninterrupted time away from her, it wasn't hard to see how toxic staying with her had been.

"Yeah," he said with a grin. "She's gonna have to pay a two-hundred-dollar replacement fee too. Marcy at the shop doesn't fuck around."

"I'm not even going to ask how you know how much someone gets charged for a ruined costume rental."

"Probably wise," he agreed. "But the bitch deserves it for how she treated Charley and Hazel at the party. If she hadn't left when I escorted her to the door, *the second time,* I would have had Mikey throw her ass out."

"What did she do?" I asked between clenched teeth, the leather on the steering wheel creaking underneath my harsh grip.

"I'll tell you once we get to your place. Don't need you getting pissed and driving us off the road."

The rest of the drive I fumed as I let myself imagine what Viv had said to my sister and my... I wasn't sure what Charley was, but she was mine.

Charley hadn't said a word when we'd talked about Viv, and part of me was pissed she hadn't told me, but the other part respected that while she'd made her distaste for my ex known, she hadn't tried to kick the rotting corpse of our long dead relationship. After the second time she'd been brought up, we'd never talked about her again.

As we drove to my house, Reid kept talking about other things that'd happened at the party after I left, spending a suspiciously long time criticizing the *pretty boy baseball player* who had apparently asked Hazel for her phone number and danced way too close to be respectful—in his opinion—to my baby sister all night.

"You seem kind of *rough* this morning, not gonna lie. Did things not go well after you guys got up there?"

"No. They went a little too well."

"That good, huh? I told you that you were attracted to her. Seems like someone finally pulled their head out of their ass and tapped that hot piece of..."

"Don't fucking talk about her like that."

"Geez, I didn't even say anything bad," he chuckled, knowing I'd get riled up by him baiting me. "What is going on with you?"

"I think I'm in love with her."

He was quiet for a beat, his voice incredulous. "After three fucking days? Does she have a pot of gold hidden inside her vagina?"

"Reid," I growled, pulling into my garage and turning off the engine.

"Okay, okay. Wrong holiday."

"Fuck off. It's not like I just met her three days ago. But now I feel like a piece of shit. She's Haz's best friend. What if I just fucked up their friendship? What if she realizes she doesn't want me?"

"Do you think she feels the same way about you?"

Contemplating my answer as we walked into the house, I went straight for the kitchen and pulled out two beers, nodding toward the living room. We spent a lot of time shooting the shit on my covered deck that looked out at the woods, but it was covered with snow.

"I don't know. I think so, but we never really made concrete plans for what happens next. I told her I'd come over after I got cleaned up, but we both have to work tonight. How am I going to spend an entire shift with her while I feel like this?"

He popped the top of his bottle, taking a swig before he responded. "You fuck her first, and then you fuck her again once you close tonight. The wall in the storeroom is pretty sturdy."

"Fuck off, asshole. No more fucking in my bar," I laughed.

"I didn't do it again...*Friday* night." The scary thing was, I couldn't tell if he was joking or not. The dude got off on fucking around in public places.

"No, you sick fuck. Not any night. Or I'm gonna come rub my balls all over your desk."

"No, you're not," he laughed. "Cause you know my balls have been naked on that desk way too many times for me to give a fuck."

"Classy," I scoffed, knowing that he wasn't lying. But he'd been right before. He was single and if women were into his slutty ways, he could take advantage of it.

"Just sayin'. It's seen some things."

Some things I was disgustingly curious about because now that my adventurous streak had been re-awoken, I might want to try some things with Charley, but ew. I didn't need to think about Reid's pale ass.

"You're disgusting. You have an apartment above the shop."

"It's seen some things too. But I thought we agreed you weren't going to slut shame me anymore, Mr. Masked Kidnapper."

"Fuck," I groaned, knowing he would use that against me at some point. I just thought he'd keep it in his pocket to bring up later.

"You're lucky your girl got a text off to Hazel before you left. Or your weekend might not have been as enjoyable." I hadn't even thought about it until the next morning, but thankfully *my girl* was smart enough to know Haz would lose her shit if she couldn't find her at the end of the night.

"Hazel is gonna kill me. She seemed weirdly calm about it when she texted me this morning, but she's scary when she's pissed."

"Haz's adorable," he laughed.

"Keep my sister's name out of your mouth." I didn't like the tone of his voice when he talked about her lately. He was like her older brother; he shouldn't think my sister was adorable. Although Charley should be like a little sister to me, but she was definitely not after what we'd done to each other this weekend.

"She's like a tiny kitten. With razor sharp claws that she wanted to use to eviscerate Viv on Friday when she came after Charley. But she got in one good bat barrel to the crotch that had half the bar cheering."

"Fuck. Why won't she just go away?" Viv was the one who didn't want me.

"I thought you wanted her to stick around?" he joked, but I was not in the mood to remember how desperate I was last week. I'd been trying to understand how a relationship that started as a six-month *friend with benefits* situationship had settled into me being her accessory boyfriend for years.

"Fuck you."

"Love has made you grumpier," he laughed, but I needed to get back to the bar so I could talk to Char. She would pull me out of this mood.

"Get the fuck out of my house. I've got shit to do," I growled, only half serious.

"Are you sure you got laid this weekend? Because you're not acting like you did."

"Get out." I pointed at the door again.

"Seriously dude, just tell her how you feel. You know she feels the same way. That girl has had hearts in her eyes when she looks at you for years. It just took you for-fucking-ever to figure it out."

I wanted to deny what he said, but Charley had already told me about her crush. I just wished I'd been observant enough to notice. Not that I'd have ever acted on it.

"What did Viv do? Might as well just tell me and get it over with."

He sighed, scratching the back of his neck. "She cornered Charley in the hallway and stabbed her with her fingernails while she insulted her because she was dressed up as the psychotic version of Harley Quinn. She accused Char of copying her. Now that I think of it, that fugly Joker costume she left on your porch makes sense. At least you dodged those bullets. I definitely would have made fun of you for that costume."

"And what did Charley do?" I couldn't imagine her taking that well. And I was now pissed she hadn't told me about it. The girl's protective streak was going to kill me.

"I stepped in between them before Charley hit her with the pink baseball bat she had to match her costume. Dragged Viv to the front door and told her to go somewhere else."

Nodding, I was thankful I had such great friends. Because Reid saving Charley meant that she was on the dance floor moments later for me to find.

"And she came back?"

He nodded. "Like a raging case of herpes."

I motioned for him to go on as he laughed at his own joke.

"I found her yelling at Hazel about someone stealing your car wearing a mask ten minutes later. When Haz ignored her, she grabbed her hair and tried to pull her back to tell her where you went, but your sister grabbed Charley's bat off a table and shoved it into her crotch, telling her to get the fuck out and not come back. I helped Mikey get her out of there with a warning we'd call the police if she came back, and we had the guys at the door keep her from coming back."

Reid had a stupid, nostalgic grin on his face, his voice filled with pride at my sister's violence toward my ex. I wasn't sure if he was excited because of Hazel, or that Viv got kicked out of the bar.

"Thank you for taking care of it. I'm sorry you had to deal with that."

"I'm not," he laughed, tilting his bottle back to swallow the rest of his drink. "Hopefully, she'll stay away from you in the future."

But after I got cleaned up, and we headed back to the bar, I had confirmation she had no intention of listening to their warnings.

Chapter
Twenty-Two

Charley

T HE BACK DOOR TO the bar slammed closed behind me, the emergency bar digging into my back as I rested my head against the cold metal. The rational part of my brain knew I'd see him in a few hours, and that this wasn't the end of the world, but the irrational part of my brain had my breath catching because my chest felt too tight. Before I knew it tears were rolling down my cheeks as I tried to hold back a sob.

There was no way that the last three days were real. There was no way that I was now actually *in love* with my best friend's brother, much less that he seemed to feel just as deeply for me.

It'd felt so natural that the panic building inside me didn't make sense, but I couldn't stop it from building.

Thankfully, the first shift for the bar wouldn't come in until eleven, so I was alone downstairs while I tried to keep myself from falling apart.

I knew we couldn't stay in the cabin forever, but when he told me the road was clear this morning, I'd been gutted, even though I was the one trying to comfort his dampened mood. We hadn't fucked this morning. Not that what we'd done together since Friday had been purely fucking, but when he took me to his bed one last time, breathing in my scent, committing my curves to memory with his large hands, his tongue reverent on my clit until it pulsed against his tongue instead of frantic with need, I knew that he was making love to me.

No one had ever made love to me before. I'd never wanted someone to either. But now I wanted it again. To feel him pinning me to the bed as his body and mine were indistinguishable, moving together until we both couldn't hold back.

The sound of a thump and a high-pitched squeak from upstairs confirmed my suspicions that Hazel was upstairs waiting for me. I knew Hudson had texted her this morning, but I'd been afraid to reach out to her.

She seemed okay when I left with him after the party, but a lot had changed over the weekend.

Taking a deep breath, I wiped my cheeks as I exhaled slowly, trying to calm myself down. She'd know something was up if she saw evidence of me crying. And I wasn't even sure why I was crying at this point.

Maybe I was just scared because this was the first time real feelings had been involved when it came to a man. I never expected that man to be Hudson, despite my long-term crush. He'd always seemed unattainable, and now that I had him, I was afraid to lose him so soon.

Once I'd double checked my face in the mirror in the ladies' bathroom, I slowly trudged up the stairs, the third stair from the top creaking. The door flew open before I could even put my hand on the knob, Hazel's somber face narrowing as she studied my face.

"You look disgustingly relaxed for someone who just spent the last three days stuck in a cabin in the middle of nowhere with my annoying older brother."

Exhaling, I grinned, stepping inside as she moved back, using my snow boot to push it closed.

"You told me you didn't want details." And even though I'd shared details of previous conquests with her before, I wanted to keep what happened with Hudson private.

"I still don't, but I guess the fact you practically floated in here means that things went well?" She looked like she knew something I didn't, her expression hopeful. It helped relax some of my earlier nerves. Maybe they *had* talked about me this morning.

"Very well," I grinned.

Hazel gagged, faking a dry heave. "Ew, but also aww..."

An uncharacteristic blush rose high on my cheeks, and she squealed, patting the cushion next to her on the couch. She had art supplies spread across the coffee table, sketch books with pencil drawings and her tablet was open to her illustration software. A stack of papers was lying underneath it. I tilted my head, trying to figure out what body part she was trying to draw.

"Do you have a stack of penis pictures under your iPad?" Then it was her turn to blush, throwing a pillow at the table to cover her stack of apparently naughty source material.

"No. Of course not."

Trying to hold in a laugh, I sputtered. "Of course not. Clearly, your commissions are only of the G and PG variety."

Her face turned an impressive shade of red and I couldn't hold it in any longer, clutching my stomach as I laughed loudly.

"It's not funny," she hissed, kicking my leg with her bare foot. "The only penis I've seen in real life was covered in a condom and not even hard anymore."

Wait, what?

"Did I just hear that right? Reid's penis is the only one you've seen up close?"

"Well, it wasn't that close, and it was dark, and I was bleeding profusely...but yes?"

"Wow."

"Shut up. This isn't about me and my lack of firsthand penis knowledge. This is about whatever is going on with Hudson. Where is he? I thought you two would be attached at the cro..."

"Hazel," I scolded. "No crotch talk if you don't want details."

She giggled, but raised an eyebrow, not letting me off the hook. And she deserved to know what was going on. Hazel had more at stake than either Hudson or me. She could potentially lose a friend or a brother if things went wrong between us. But I'd never make her choose.

"He's coming in later to catch up with the staff who's on tonight to make sure they're ready to open." At least that's what I hoped he still planned on doing.

"Then I'm sure Mikey will fill him in on how the shit hit the fan right after you guys left." Hazel scowled, her hands clenching at her sides, and I had a feeling that psycho Harley had made a reappearance after Hudson drove away with me tied up in his back seat.

"What happened? Did someone get into a fight?"

"Yeah," she laughed. "I guess you could say that. Viv cornered me and started yelling about someone stealing Hudson's car. I guess she saw it leaving the lot when she came back after getting escorted out the first time, and she wanted to know where he went. I knew it was Hudson leaving with you since I'd just read your last text message and refused to tell her. She lost it when I told her that Hudson didn't leave alone, and Reid came over to rescue me. When she tried to pull my off my halo with a chunk of my hair, I grabbed the bat you left behind on the table and shoved it into her twat."

I choked out a laugh at her usage of the word *twat,* but I was proud of my friend for sticking up for herself.

"Mikey had to drag her out to the parking lot to cool off. And then sent her home with her friends when Reid threatened to call the cops. She saw me watching the whole thing and warned me she'd be back for answers later."

"Fuck," I sighed, knowing that it was inevitable Viv would show up at some point. She'd basically told Hudson that she wanted him to wait around while she hooked up with other guys to make sure she actually wanted him. Which I told him was bullshit, because he was a catch and if she didn't realize that she was stupider than I thought she was, but he wasn't hers anymore.

"You don't think he'd go back to her, do you?"

"Fuck no," I hissed. But I wasn't entirely sure. My heart said he wouldn't, but she'd manipulated him for years. Other than our brief conversations about how she'd mistreated him, he hadn't brought her up again. We'd been too busy doing *other things* with our mouths to waste words on her.

"Are you two dating?"

Pausing, I tried to figure out how to answer her. We'd spent the entire drive back this morning holding hands, but he'd never actually said where he wanted things to go from where we'd left them. He'd implied that things would continue once we were back home, but I'd been disappointed by promises made in the heat of the moment before. It was why I'd never committed to a relationship after undergrad.

Was I just a fling? Did the forced proximity of the storm heighten things unrealistically between us?

"Shit. You're gonna freak out now, aren't you? Do I need to go beat some sense into him?"

That was the last thing I needed. Hazel could be fierce when she was pissed off, and I didn't want this to drive a wedge between them. Hudson hadn't defined things between us, but the kiss he'd laid on me once we'd parked behind the bar had to mean he didn't want this to be over.

"No. No..." My knee shook as I tried not to let the panic overtake me.

"I'll fucking kill him," she growled, pushing up from the couch.

I grabbed her arm, pulling her back down beside me. "No, you're not going to kill him. I just need to talk to him."

"He should have fucking told you what he wanted *before* you two came back here. You two have to be the shittiest communicators on the planet. Spend 72 hours snowed into a remote cabin and neither one of you thought to come up for air and talk about this?"

"The whole thing was an accident. You think we were concerned with reality when this all started?"

"La la la la..." she hummed, covering her ears. I smacked her in the arm, and she cracked up laughing, sticking her tongue out at me.

"You're the one who wants to talk about this. It's not like I told you how big his di..." her palm smacked against my mouth, cutting off my words. I licked her palm, and she narrowed her eyes at me in warning.

"Okay, okay, no talk about the size of..." I trailed off laughing at the look on her face. "I'm done. But anyway, we talked, about more than...stuff, but I was too afraid to ask him about what happened when we were forced back into reality."

"Do you want me to text Reid?" Hazel looked just as eager for answers as I was.

"You mean the guy you can't formulate complete sentences around and run the opposite way from whenever he looks in your direction?" Clearly a lot of things had changed at that party.

"He was actually surprisingly sweet after Mikey dragged Viv out of the bar. He made sure I was okay, and several times for the rest of the night I saw him watching me from across the room."

Oh, my poor, sweet oblivious friend. She spent too much time with the imaginary—apparently horny—characters in her tablet.

"Um...do you not see him watching you every night you're on shift?"

Her eyes widened, her mouth almost comically dropping open into the perfect o shape. "What? No, he doesn't."

"And I'm the one who needs to pay attention to their surroundings," I muttered, remembering Hudson's first words to me on the dance floor.

"He doesn't really do that, does he? I look like shit half the time after a shift when it gets crazy down there. What if he caught me picking my nose? Oh my God."

"I mean, not *all* the time, but I've definitely caught him watching you lately. I think he's trying to figure out why you won't talk to him... And why you run away whenever he enters the room."

"You know why I'm hiding," she hissed, covering her face with her hands. Her voice dropped to a scandalized whisper. "I've seen his penis."

"I think a lot of people have seen Reid's penis," I giggled.

"You're not helping," she pouted. "You think I like having a crush on my brother's philandering best friend?"

"He hasn't been that bad lately."

Reid had spent just as much time as he ever had in the bar, but most nights he was here helping until closing time, not over in his shop banging random women.

"He's had more sex in the last month than I've had like ever."

"That just means you know he'd show you a good time if you'd stop running from him."

"Yeah right," she scoffed. "Or he'd laugh in my face if he knew I liked him. I'm not exactly his type."

"Well, I didn't think I was Hudson's. But that didn't stop him from fuc..."

"I hate you," she laughed, slapping her hand across my mouth.

"No, you don't. You love me."

She grinned before she reached over to open her cell phone, thrusting it in my face with the text conversation from this morning up on the screen. "And so does my brother."

Chapter Twenty-Three

Charley

HAZEL ENCOURAGED ME TO get cleaned up and ready for my shift while she continued to work on her lewd sketches before she had an appointment later today. If she thought Hudson was protective now, I knew he could never learn about the turn her illustration commissions had taken.

Apparently if the characters had their clothes off, then she got paid twice as much. I admired the entrepreneurial spirit, but it was kind of comical knowing my virginal best friend was drawing naughty illustrations to pay her bills.

I kind of wanted to commission a naughty UNO inspired deck from her, but that might be crossing way too many boundaries with all parties involved. Hudson would be into the cards but mortified that his sister knew we'd defiled her favorite childhood game. Hazel would be grossed out by all the above. And I'd have to describe sexual positions to my best friend so she could illustrate them because she didn't have any first-hand knowledge.

Maybe she had some other naughty artist friends I could hit up with my idea.

By the time I got downstairs, the bar had opened but we only had a few patrons seated in their usual spots. Once they were served, they usually kept to themselves, so I sat down at the other end to chat with Annie. I wanted to make sure there hadn't been any more drama over the weekend.

"So, you are alive," she teased, sliding a glass of water in front of me. I took a long drink, knowing I was probably dehydrated from all the fluids I'd expelled over the weekend. "Hazel said she'd heard from you, but when Hudson wasn't anywhere to be found and you were both gone all weekend, the gossip started."

"How bad is it?" I cringed, hating that we'd been a topic of discussion among my co-workers. But they were bound to figure it out fairly quickly when they saw Hudson and I interact.

"The cooks have a bet going that Hudson will mysteriously disappear because you disposed of his body in the woods after being snowed in with him for three days."

"He is alive and well. Or at least he was a few hours ago."

"That's what I figured. The waitstaff has an over under on how many times you guys fucked over the weekend. Apparently, they've been getting sexual tension vibes off you two for months. They were just waiting for him to kick Viv to the curb and realize you were a better suited match."

"How exactly did they plan on verifying that?" I laughed, knowing that neither of us had really kept a count, but I wasn't planning to tell them anyway. Maybe the slight limp when I walked would clue them in that we didn't spend the entire weekend playing checkers.

"I think they were hoping for one of you to slip. Hell, just make up a random number and have Hazel bet, then you can clear them all out for being nosy bastards."

"Anything else? Did the she-witch show back up?"

She laughed, knowing exactly who I was referring to.

"No, after Hazel using your bat for the money shot and Reid toting her ass to the parking lot screaming so loudly he threatened to call the cops, none of us saw her again."

Thank God.

"Do you think she's going to come back now that the weather has cleared?"

She shrugged, wiping away the sweat ring my glass had left on the bar. "That chick is seriously delulu, there's no telling what she'll do. But I thought her head was going to explode when Hazel insinuated that he left with you. So, you might want to watch your back."

Great. Just what I needed, a psycho ex stalking me because I stole her boy toy. Now that he wasn't drinking her Kool Aid anymore, she was clearly panicking that she'd actually have to be a nice person to attract another man. Although some guys were into harpies, maybe she'd luck out and find one of them to train.

"Fuck," Annie hissed, slowly darting her eyes toward the door to the bar.

Shifting slightly, I leaned over to look at the mirror behind Annie which reflected the front door. I should have known by the cold draft and the sense of dread slowly creeping up my spine that talking about her had summoned her evil ass.

"What's she doing?" I whispered, paying more attention than warranted to my glass of water.

"She's wiping down the menu with a hand sanitizer wipe she pulled out of her purse." Annie curled her lip and shook her head. "Now she's turning the pages like she's going to catch an incurable disease from the laminated pages."

"Ugh. She's so annoying."

"Now she's glaring over here, snapping her fingers in the air."

"Does she think you're her servant or something? I don't understand this entitled shit. Her father runs the fucking discount shoe store in Butterfly Ridge, it's not like she's royalty."

"I think she noticed you. She just moved to a closer table and is typing something furiously into her phone. I don't know how anyone can type with fake nails that long. They look like talons. And they probably have more bacteria than the menu did. How do you even wipe your ass with those things on?"

I stifled a laugh, recalling the several inch long fake nails she was poking me with at the party. She must've had to drive to Pueblo to get those things done, because I knew the local nail techs didn't do those.

"What should I do? Should I try to sneak out?"

"Fuck no," she laughed, continuing to ignore the woman who was now audibly huffing behind me. "Maybe you should *accidentally* tell me all about your weekend with our naughty boss."

"Ann, really? I don't kiss and tell…much. Hudson tries so hard to be professional, I don't want him to think I'm gossiping about our private business to my co-workers who are his employees."

"It's me. You know I'm not going to say anything, and I think *bitchella* needs a little wake-up call that Hudson has upgraded. And judging by the marks, you didn't do a very good job of covering, he's a bit of an animal in the sack."

Subtly glancing over my shoulder, I made sure Viv was listening before I raised my voice. "Oh my God, I didn't know he could be like that. Like, I know he's our boss, but that man is seriously dirty. The mouth on him. Fuck."

"Sounds like someone had a better weekend than I did. I was stuck here covering for your ass while you were off screwing Hudson."

"And I don't regret a second of it. It was so worth all the tips I lost." And it really was. No amount of bar tips would offset the feeling of Hudson pressing me down and whispering dirty things in my ear as he fucked orgasm after orgasm out of my body. "I'm so tired, but I guess that many orgasms in just a few days would make anyone exhausted."

Annie sputtered, her lip quivering with suppressed laughter before she got control of herself. "Looks like it. I don't think I've ever seen you this relaxed."

"It kind of hurts to sit down," I chuckled, pushing my hair over my shoulder to make sure that the bite marks on my neck were visible from where Viv sat behind me. I wished I could record the look on her face right now, but as Annie's eyes widened and she bit her lip to hold in a laugh, I knew it had to be epic. "I may need one of those donut things for like the next week. But we've got plans for later. So maybe I just need to woman up and take it like a… What did he call me? *A naughty little devil.*"

Annie's attempt to hold back the laughter cracked and I lost it with her, giggling as a growl sounded from behind me.

"Um, excuse me?" Viv's shrill voice called out, approaching the bar from behind me. "Does anyone here actually work? I've been sitting over there for five minutes and no one has come to take my drink order."

Annie rolled her eyes, throwing the bar towel she'd been holding across her shoulder. "It's a weekday, ma'am. We don't have any servers on table duty until eight. You'll need to come to the bar to place an order."

"*Fucking worthless*," she hissed under her breath, but both Annie and I heard her. "Fine. I'll take a dry martini. Do you have any top shelf liquor?"

She'd only been in this place about a million times over the last four years, and she had no idea what we carried behind the bar? "I don't want any of that cheap shit you put in the college *kids'* drinks."

Clenching my fists in my lap, I tried not to rise to her bait. She knew I was in grad school, so I had a feeling the *kids'* comment was aimed at me. I was only two years younger than her, but apparently that meant I was a child.

"We have Tito's. If you want something different, you're in the wrong bar, *ma'am.*"

"Excuse me? Does your boss know you're trying to turn away business?"

Annie had been around long before I'd been hired. She was one of the original bartenders Hudson had trained when he started working here full time straight out of college.

"Is there anything else I can get for you?" Annie growled with a strained smile that was bordering on frightening.

"Well, since everything you serve here is gross and fried, I guess just the drink. You can put it on Hudson's tab. I'm waiting for him right now. Has he come in yet? He's supposed to be back today."

"I'm sorry, *ma'am,* but Hudson doesn't allow anyone to add drinks to his *tab.* And no, he's not here yet. He had a *very, very* long weekend being stranded by the snowstorm. I'm the only bartender on shift right now."

"But he's *always* here," she pouted.

"Not right now. But I'd be happy to pass the message along that you stopped by to meet him."

"*Meet* him? He's my boyfriend," she laughed, but she sounded a bit manic.

I tried not to let the comment sting, because I knew better, but she had better be fucking wrong. Hudson hadn't acted like he was going to go running back to *bitchtastic* as soon as we got back to town.

"Hardly," I coughed under my breath and Annie shot me a look with wide eyes that I should probably keep my mouth shut. But fuck that shit.

"He'll probably be in soon," I mentioned casually. "He was planning to take a nap because he was exhausted from digging out the drive from the main road to the cabin this morning."

"And you know this how?" Viv asked, leaning on the bar next to me and narrowing her eyes.

"Because I helped him."

"*You* were at the cabin with him?"

"Sure was."

"Do you make it a habit of spending the weekend snowed into cabins with other people's boyfriends? Or did you sneak up there, so he'd be stuck with you?" she asked, but judging by the daggers she was staring at my neck, she'd noticed his work. Not that it'd be familiar to her.

"Well, that would involve Hudson having a girlfriend. Last time I checked, he was single. *For now.* Someone decided last week that it was better if they *explored their options*. And Hudson spent the weekend exploring the *fuck* out of his. He explored so hard he almost blacked out once."

"Uh," she sputtered, her face turning red. I watched as her fingers balled into fists, her knuckles turning white. "Look, *Cherrie*, or whatever the fuck your name is. Hudson and I are *not* on a break. He's been my boyfriend for four years. We're planning on moving in together after Christmas and I've already picked out a ring for him. I'm willing to overlook whatever you think happened this week, but you better start packing now, because I'm going to make sure you're completely gone from his life and this building. Erasing a *nobody* won't be very hard."

Spinning on my stool to face her, I stood, looming over her in my platform combat boots. We may have been built similarly, but I sure as fuck wasn't going to let her talk to me like this. Things may be uncertain with Hudson, but one thing I was absolutely certain of was that he deserved better than this manipulative bitch.

"Listen here, you thundercun—" my voice cut off as a palm covered my mouth. My body was suddenly crushed against a hard chest, Hudson's familiar comforting scent wafting over me.

"Viv, that's enough," he growled, the menacing tone from when he'd chased me through the woods returning, sending goose bumps crawling up my spine. "You've been told to stay away twice now and chosen to ignore it, should we make it a third time? Because if you don't leave, I *am* going to call the cops. And then I'm going to have *both* Hazel and Charley file harassment complaints against you assaulting them in my bar. I doubt your boss would like to hear about the protective order I file next for stalking."

"But..." she whimpered, her eyes as wide as saucers as they bounced between his possessive hold on me and his face. "Your sister hit me with a bat. I could sue."

"Self-defense," Annie chimed in. "I saw the whole thing and already pulled the camera footage. It clearly shows you yanking Hazel's hair and dragging her away from a table before she was forced to use the bat to get you to let go."

I was so sad I didn't get to witness it in person.

"And I'm not stalking you, I just want to talk to you. Clearly, you misunderstood our conversation last week. Because I..."

Hudson cut her off with a growl. "You made your decision—the bullshit you fed me was perfectly fucking clear—and I sure as fuck made mine. Get out. You're trespassing."

"But this is a public bar and I'm a paying customer..."

Annie cut in again. "Technically, you haven't paid yet. But you still have an outstanding tab from the last two times you were here. I'm sure the police would love to add a misdemeanor for failing to pay a bill for services rendered to the felonies of assault and harassment."

I almost felt sorry for the way Viv was looking at him. She'd obviously felt very strongly about him at one point, but that time was over. She'd thrown him to the curb like a piece of garbage because this sweet and responsible man wasn't exciting enough for her. If she only knew what he was truly capable of back then, but now she never would.

"Get the fuck out," he growled again, his hand slipping from my mouth to possessively cup my neck. "I don't want to ever see you in here again. And stay away from my house. My doorbell camera caught your car driving by twenty times over the last three days, so that should help with the restraining order paperwork."

"I need to talk to you," she hissed, her earlier surprise morphing into anger. "You can't just kick me out."

"I can," he laughed, pointing toward the door with his other hand. I tried not to swoon as I watched the tendons in his forearm flex enticingly. Even pissed off at his ex this man made my pulse race. "Because you've done nothing but disrespect me, my business and my employees for days. And *no one* talks to my woman like that."

"But she..."

"She didn't fucking do anything, Viv. I took her to the cabin—where she actually loved spending time with *me*—and I *chose* to spend the weekend with her. And I'm choosing her now. I should have chosen her a long time ago."

"Did you cheat on me with this..." she sucked in air before she hissed out. "...this home wrecking *whore.*"

"The only time Charley is a whore is in my bed, Viv. And believe me, it's all consensual and she *loves* it."

My face turned red as I watched Viv's previous ire transform into pure rage. But Hudson just chuckled, leaning down to kiss my cheek. Guess I didn't need to worry about him being upset about me telling people details about our bedroom habits.

Before I could anticipate the move, he spun me around and hoisted me against his chest. "I'm sorry," he mouthed before he leaned over me and pressed my back against the bar. His eyes softened as he looked down at me. I opened my mouth to ask him what was going on and he captured my words with his lips, grasping both cheeks with his strong hands and forcing his tongue past my lips.

It took me a moment to catch up, kissing him back just as fiercely as my hands dove into his hair, gripping tightly.

The shriek that sounded a few feet from us, followed by the stomping of heels and the door to the bar slamming didn't even register as we devoured each other.

Chapter
Twenty-Four

"ALRIGHT, YOU CAN COME up for air now," Annie laughed. Hudson let out a yelp as she cracked a bar towel against his bicep just inches from my face. "She's gone. And I hope for the last time. But I do have footage of her cornering Charley and the fight with Hazel saved on your laptop if you need it."

"I hope she's gone too," I murmured, studying the intense look on his face for signs of whether or not that kiss was just for show.

"She is," he assured, leaning down to peck my lips, lingering to brush his tenderly across mine. "Long gone."

"You might want to take this somewhere more private," Annie urged, nodding her head toward the back.

The sound of the door of the bar opening and closing had Hudson pulling away from me, but my hand was in his and I was being tugged toward his office before I could react.

He didn't stop as he passed his closed door, pulling me behind him and turning the corner to the back storage room.

"Where are you taking me?" I laughed, unused to seeing him so amped up when he wasn't trying to LARP a masked kidnapper.

"Wherever I want," he growled, then stopped suddenly and hoisted me over his shoulder.

"You know I can walk, right?" I giggled, the blood rushing to my head as I hung upside down over his shoulder.

"Not for long."

"Oh, really? Sounds like a big promise. You sure you can handle it after your *activities* this weekend? Might need to take your vitamins and get some rest, old man."

"I think we both know my recovery time is accelerated the second your clothes start coming off. Or at least your panties. If you're wearing any. Which you better fucking be."

My body bounced as he headed up the back staircase to my apartment with a possessive hand on my ass, and I was thankful that Hazel had left earlier after we talked.

We were going to have to work out some kind of signal, so she didn't walk in on another traumatizing coupling. While I knew she supported whatever was developing with Hudson, I doubted she'd want to hear things sisters aren't meant to hear.

He stopped on the landing in front of my door and fished around in his pocket, pulling out his keys to the building.

"You know you're supposed to notify us before you come inside the apartment. Just because you're the bossman around here doesn't mean you can do whatever you want."

"Consider this your notification that I absolutely plan to come inside your apartment—and you. Multiple times if you're up for it."

"I think you're the one who's supposed to be *up* for it," I teased.

He kicked the door open, and it bounced off the wall with a thud.

"Hey! I'm not paying for that if you dented our wall."

"I'm the one who fixes that shit anyway. If I want to dent the wall, I'll dent the fucking wall. About to put a fucking hole in the one behind your headboard next."

"Too late for dents," I laughed.

"Yeah, tell me about it. Fucking lucky bastards."

He tossed me onto the end of my bed before he crossed back to the door, flipping the lock.

"What is that supposed to mean?" I asked, leaning back on my palms.

He stalked toward me, pulling off his shirt and revealing his heavily inked skin. He didn't stop when he reached me, bracing his hands next to mine, and leaning in close to my face.

"It means I know exactly how you dented your wall."

"You were serious that you could hear it?"

"Yes," he whispered, leaning in to kiss me. "This bedroom is directly above my office. It wasn't just a line when I said you deserved more than the one-night stands you bring up here."

"I'm sorry. I thought you were just teasing me. If I would have known you actually heard..."

"Honestly don't give a fuck, we both have pasts that we need to leave there. *But* I'll be the only reason you dent that wall from now on. I may even fix it and then see how much damage *I* can do to it."

"Sounds a little possessive. What if I want to give someone else a shot at it?"

I didn't, but I also still wasn't sure if this was more than a fling.

"Don't fucking test me, Charley. You know you're mine."

"No, actually," I whispered, cupping his jaw, and rubbing my thumb over the scruff on his cheek. "I don't know. Because we never talked about what comes next."

"You," he breathed, pressing forward until I was flat against the mattress. "You're what comes next."

"Oh," I moaned as his teeth scraped down the side of my neck, Hudson nipping at the teeth marks he'd left behind. "But what if you decide it was just temporary? What happens once the novelty of fucking your little sister's best friend wears off?"

"Don't bring up Haz while I'm trying to get you naked. But you don't need to worry about that. You're all I want in my future. And not just this fucking sinful body," he whispered, lifting the hem of my tank top, and kissing my stomach, his tongue swirling in my belly button. "I want your smart mouth, and the way you challenge me. Those eyes that cut right through me."

A moan was my only response as he flicked the button on my jeans open dragging down the zipper with his teeth.

"I want to spend my nights worshiping this pussy, and every morning waking up to your horrible alarms. I can hear those in my office too."

"Mmm," I hummed as he peeled off my jeans, taking my thong down with them and blindly throwing them behind him. He leaned in, closing his eyes and inhaling deeply.

"I want to spend all my free time with you. I want to watch you throw unruly frat boys out of my bar when they touch what's mine. I want to help support you when you need it, and even when you don't. I want to find a place in here..." His palm covered my heart, and I sniffled, tears cropping up in the corners of my eyes. "And have Reid tattoo my name on your ass or maybe your tits. I haven't decided yet."

"Um. No," I giggled, but the thought didn't seem so unappealing at the moment.

"We can negotiate that later. Maybe I'll just get you a necklace with my name on it."

"What if it wasn't real?" I choked out, trying not to laugh at the idea of him standing guard and glaring at his best friend while he inked Hudson's name on my ass.

"I may have lost my shit when you walked out of my bathroom at the cabin," he started, laying his head across my stomach.

"Just a little," I whispered, combing my fingers through his hair.

"But once I got over the fact that I accidentally kidnapped my little sister's best friend, I knew I didn't want to spend another moment away from you. Things should have been awkward, but they weren't, and I felt like you actually gave a shit about what I had to say when we talked. Playing games and laughing with you in the dark was the most fun I've had in years."

"But you just dropped me off here and left without saying anything about where we go from here."

"Because I was afraid I'd say something stupid, and you'd realize all of this wasn't worth your time. But then when I walked through the kitchen and saw you ready to literally fight for me, and I couldn't stay away from you anymore."

"I don't want you to. But I wasn't sure if I was reason enough to stay."

He growled, surging forward, tucking his hands into my armpits, and hoisting me into the center of my bed. "You are more than a fucking reason. And I'm sorry it took me so long to see what has been right in front of me for far too long. You're all I want now. You're all I see. And it's time I started showing you that."

Chapter
Twenty-Five

Hudson

T HIS GIRL—THIS AMAZINGLY SEXY and brilliant woman—really
had no idea how much of a chokehold she had on me.

My first instinct when she came out of that bathroom a few days
ago may have been to lose my absolute shit, but it hadn't been
because I wasn't attracted to her. Even when I tried to push it down,
I'd known how gorgeous she was for years inside and out, and while
we often butted heads, her devious mind was just as attractive as
the outside package.

Before I'd gotten to know her, the age difference had seemed
like a much larger deal than it really was. But there were six years
between my parents, and they'd never let a little age gap get in the
way of their relationship. My mom had barely turned twenty-one
when she'd met him downstairs in this bar. And the way my dad
told it, she'd burrowed a hole in his heart and refused to leave from
that moment on.

That was how I felt about Charley.

Last week I fooled myself into thinking I'd been devastated that
Viv had broken things off, but her letting me go had been a relief.
Because even though I thought I was enacting her fantasy during
the party, I'd really been carrying out mine. The one where I did
what I wanted without worry of criticism.

Charley pushed me to step outside the boundaries I'd created
for myself, and I wanted her to keep doing it. I wanted her to push
me.

Right now, I wanted to push something else inside of her, but she really had no idea how much she'd shaken the foundation of my reality in a few short days.

"You have no fucking idea how much you destroyed me, and then helped put me right back together. I don't want this to end. Not now, maybe not ever."

"Are you sure? Because I think it'd break me if you decided this isn't what you want once the sex haze wears off."

She had no idea the thought of walking away from her made parts of my heart I hadn't even known existed ache. And I was just as scared of her walking away from me. We hadn't talked about her plans once she graduated, and I was terrified there wouldn't be a place in her life for me once she wasn't stuck here for grad school.

"Then let's never let it wear off. I don't think I'll ever stop craving you now. And no, I'm not just talking about your body. I'm talking about *you*. Who you are as a person. I don't ever want the haze of you to wear off." Her eyes were brimming with tears as she combed her fingers through my hair. I hated that I'd made her question how strong my feelings had become for her.

Because even though we still had a lot to learn about each other, I felt like she actually cared who I was, not who she could mold me to be. I hadn't realized how much that'd been missing from my life. Viv had been so obsessed with shoving me into a neat little box that I'd lost sight of myself. And I refused to climb back in that fucking box.

"Now, can I take off these clothes? Because I'm dying to get you completely naked. We both have to work in a few hours, and I don't think I can survive until tomorrow morning if I don't make you come in the next two minutes."

"Well, I don't want you to die, so..." she teased, grasping the hem of her tank top and pulling it upward.

Leaning back, I pulled it over her head and threw it somewhere behind me. I took a long look at her, groaning when her bare breasts came into view. "You really need to start wearing bras and panties or I'm never going to get anything done because I'm going to want to fuck you constantly."

"And that's a bad thing?" Her fingers plucked at her already hard nipples, and my mouth watered at the thought of taking them into my mouth.

"You can walk around my house naked for all I care, but when we're at work, I'm going to need you to behave yourself. No one will come to drink anymore if I kick them all out or hit them over the head with beer bottles for staring at my girlfriend's nipples."

"So, I'm your girlfriend now?" she whispered, pulling my head forward.

"Mmhmm," I hummed, latching onto her nipple, sucking hard and enjoying the way her back arched, pushing her naked body against me.

"What if I don't want to be your girlfriend?"

My body froze, a sense of panic running through me, but the tilt of her lips clued me in that she wasn't serious.

"Then I'm just going to have to kidnap you again and keep you in my cabin until you come to your senses. I'm thinking if I keep up the orgasms, it won't take you long to come around. Think of it like sexy Stockholm Syndrome. I'll have you dickmatized in no time."

When she laughed, my body relaxed, my hands roaming hers as I kissed every inch of her soft, exposed skin. I'd been afraid when we left this morning that I'd never get to take my time to explore her again. That something in real life would threaten to pull us apart. But Charley had been more than willing to put my ex in her place to stake her claim on me, and I wasn't going to question that. Because if the situation was reversed, her ex would have been on the ground in the parking lot with more than a wounded ego.

She hissed as I slid inside, despite the fact that she was ridiculously wet.

"You okay, baby? I don't want to hurt you."

Her eyes were soft, the intensity of her hazel hued gaze focused squarely on me. "Just a little sore. But I want to be close to you."

"I'll be gentle," I whispered, tucking my face into her neck as I slowly rolled my hips, enjoying the way she sunk her fingernails into my back to keep me close.

"But I like it better when you're not."

"Later, baby. We've got all the time in the world for me to fuck you raw until you're sitting funny for days. And to leave reminders of just how hungry I am for you on your skin," I growled into her neck, leaving a trail of teasing kisses behind instead of bite marks on my way to her luscious mouth.

"I love your marks."

And I love you, I thought as I slipped my hand behind her neck, gripping the sides and kissing her as I made love to her for the second time, exhaling in relief when she clenched around me minutes later, my release filling her when I couldn't hold off any longer.

Because I had absolutely no self-control around this woman, and I wasn't sure I ever wanted to.

Epilogue

Hudson

"**O**H *FUCK*, HARDER! G O harder! Hit me like you mean it," she screamed, her legs tensing as I lifted my hand, flicking my wrist and watching as little red welts rose on the creamy skin of her ass with each pass of the leather tails on the flogger clutched in my fist.

The fire crackled on the other side of the room, and I still couldn't believe this was my life. That the insanely hot naked woman draped across my lap was mine, and that in a few days, she'd be moving into my house.

Four months ago, I couldn't imagine sharing my space with someone—the *who* in mind I wouldn't even name because she wasn't worth taking up space in my head—and now I couldn't wait until I could wake up with her in my arms every morning.

Charley had been worried about what would happen with Hazel when I asked her to move in with me, but she'd been surprisingly cool with it. Haz was already picking out a huge wrap-around desk with a built-in drafting table to turn her bestie's old room into her studio space.

When I found out she'd been talking with our parents to put an addition onto the back of the bar for her to have a drawing studio to work in as her custom illustration business grew, it seemed like it was the perfect time. I was tired of spending any unnecessary time away from Char because of our living arrangements.

Slipping my hand underneath Charley, my fingers slid effortlessly inside her warm, wet heat and her moans increased in pitch as I fucked her with my fingers. As much as I got a rush from giving it, we'd discovered that she came the hardest after I inflicted a little bit of pain.

She'd been hiding a secret stash of toys from me for months and was mortified when I'd found the locked box underneath her bed while we were packing her room. I'd assumed it was important documents or something, but it was full of things she'd accumulated over the last few years and had been afraid to use with a partner.

When she'd suggested sneaking away to the cabin for the weekend to celebrate Valentine's Day a few weeks early, I'd jumped at the chance to spend the weekend naked together defiling more of the place where we'd discovered how well we worked together as a couple.

"Are you close, baby? I'm dying here," I groaned, palming my aching cock beneath my boxer briefs.

"One more time," she begged breathlessly, her fingers digging into the couch cushion next to her face while she braced for the impact.

"Last time," I panted. "Then I'm fucking you until you soak the couch."

I lifted my hand, teasingly trailing the tails over her reddened skin, hooking the fingers inside her to rub her in the spot I knew would have her coming all over me in seconds.

"Do it already!" she screamed, rocking her hips into the insistent movements of my fingers.

"It's still cute you think you're in charge of this," I taunted, pausing my hand, and smiling at the frustrated groan she muffled into the leather beneath her face.

"Please," she whimpered, clenching her pussy around my fingers in a way that had me groaning and my cock throbbing. "Don't torture me like this. I need to come."

But I continued edging her, alternating slowly stroking my fingers and gently tracing the leather strands across her skin. When her pants turned into whimpers, I took pity on her, swiping my thumb over her clit and striking her ass with the tails of the flogger until she was shaking and crying out, her hips following my hand as she squeezed my fingers.

"Time for a nap, baby?" I teased as I watched her back rise and fall with labored breaths.

She had enough energy to lift her hand, aiming her middle finger at me.

"Just the invitation I was looking for," I chuckled, pulling her legs off my lap, and stretching them across the couch. I pushed my boxer briefs to the floor, groaning as I stroked my cock a few times before I threw a leg over her thighs, straddling her and aiming for her wet, tight, still pulsing pussy.

She moaned as I pushed inside, rocking back and forth a few times before I leaned over her body, bracing one hand on the arm of the couch and the other on the back of her neck. "You going to come for me again?"

Charley whimpered, but she flexed her hips into each thrust, using her hands to brace herself for the impact.

Sliding my fingers into her hair, I fisted it and pressed her face into the cushion below her, growling in her ear. "Answer me or I'll stop before you do and come all over your ass again."

While she liked me decorating her pretty, mascara-streaked face every so often, I knew she liked it more when I came inside her.

"Charley," I growled, pulling her head back and groaning when she squeezed her thighs together.

"You know I could flip you off me and leave you here to jerk off alone," she teased, but she was still out of breath.

While she'd only shown off her taekwondo moves a few times—because we'd gotten distracted and fucked before she could show me more—I knew she was more than capable of throwing me around.

"I know you'd just stand in the hallway and watch me. Because you're my dirty little whore."

"Fuck," she groaned, trying to push her hips into mine. She liked it when I called her names.

"My filthy little cum slut who loves it when I make her dirty," I continued, growling when she squeezed me again.

"And who is so fucking cock hungry that she drags me back to my office and swallows my cum while we should be working with the door unlocked so anyone could catch her on her knees for me."

Slowly rocking my hips, I kept whispering things in her ear, her whimpers increasing in pitch until she was moaning and coming all over me again soaking my thighs with her release. Stars danced in my field of vision when I finally let go, emptying myself inside her.

"Now it's nap time," she giggled as I pulled out of her, my cum leaking onto the leather cushion underneath her hips. I trailed my finger through it, enjoying the gasp she let out when I carefully pressed it all back inside.

We'd had the conversation about children and our future. We wanted to enjoy the next few years together before we got married and she started popping out kids. She was going to keep taking birth control until we decided otherwise, but I still had the occasional fleeting thought about what she'd look like with her body growing my baby. Maybe she'd unlocked another kink I didn't know I had.

"Roll, baby," I whispered, climbing over her sated form, and pressing my back against the couch cushions before I gathered her in my arms.

I thought she'd fallen asleep, but her quiet voice kept me from dozing off. "Do you think the event will go okay?"

"Baby," I whispered, trying to comb my fingers through the tangled hair on the back of her head. "You've been working on this for months. And I've seen all the plans every step of the way. You've got this. You didn't even need my help."

She had come to me in December with a project she'd completed the semester before during one of her classes. It was for a two-part blind speed dating event centered around Valentine's Day.

While we'd never done an event like that before, it'd garnered quite a bit of interest, and we'd spent weeks after New Year's vetting the fourteen men we selected to participate so we didn't end up with any creeps. Charley had interviewed the women with Annie, making sure to exclude the walking red flags like my ex, who had thankfully disappeared from our lives.

"Are you sure you're okay with Hazel participating? I know I kind of went after her for it, but she spends so much time alone, and I don't want her to be even lonelier once I officially move out."

"We made sure there weren't any douchebags in the bunch. I can't promise you that she'll give any of them her number, but maybe she'll meet a nice guy. She's going to need someone to keep her busy when I refuse to let you leave the bed on our days off."

"You're such a guy," she laughed, shaking her head at me, but she was just as ravenous about our sex life—which had only gotten better since we'd left here in November.

"And I think you like that about me." Pressing my hips into her, she smiled up at me as I poked her in the stomach.

"Sometimes, maybe just a little."

That was something else that hadn't changed. We had our moments where we disagreed about things, but we could still be playful with each other. Our senses of humor complemented each other, and I never once felt like I wasn't allowed to be myself.

Our parents had been happy for us too, and we spent the holidays together. Thanksgiving—where we'd held a blended family celebration at the bar—and Christmas—where her parents had come up to the cabin to celebrate with my family.

It was impossible to imagine not spending the rest of my life with this woman. And I hated that I'd been so blinded by a superficial relationship that I lost years with her. But I was also thankful for what we did have, because we'd both learned lessons with our previous partners that made us appreciate what we had.

I also never thought I'd be so grateful for a cheap ten-dollar Halloween mask. That night changed my life, and everything worked out exactly as it needed to, even if the entire night didn't go as planned.

Best accidental abduction of my life—and also, the only one. But I still wouldn't be opposed to chasing her around the woods every once in a while.

THE END

THE DIRTY WORDS SERIES

Foreplay on Words (Amazon)

Book One of The Dirty Words Series
Evan and Chase
Preview of Foreplay on Words: https://BookHip.com/WCJHJGA

Mark my Words (Amazon)

Book Two of The Dirty Words Series
Sam and Kristine
Preview of Mark my Words: https://BookHip.com/QHWGXTZ

Bound by Words (Amazon)

Book Three of The Dirty Words Series
Nathan and Kelly
Preview of Bound by Words: https://BookHip.com/NRRHRBN

More Than Words (Amazon)

Book Four of The Dirty Words Series
Adrian and Isobel
Preview of More Than Words: https://BookHip.com/TARMSTL

.

.

MASKED MEN OF SAGE SPRINGS

Accidental Abduction (Amazon)

Book One in the Masked Men of Sage Springs Series
Hudson and Charley
Preview of Accidental Abduction: https://bookhip.com/CDPWX
AB
Coming to audio soon!

Illicit Illustration (Amazon)

Book Two in the Masked Men of Sage Springs Series
Reid and Hazel
Preview of Illicit Illustration: https://bookhip.com/CDPWXAB

Smokin' Situation (Amazon)

Book Three in the Masked Men of Sage Springs Series
Annie and Tristan
Preview of Smokin' Situation: https://bookhip.com/FCDAKTZ

.

.

STANDALONES

The Midnight Voyeur (Amazon)

Now available in Duet audio featuring Branden Davis-Butler, Cole Eubanks and Troy Duran: https://books2read.com/themidnightv oyeur
(Wide at all audio retailers)
Spicy, taboo, reverse age-gap, stand-alone – Ginny
Preview The Midnight Voyeur: https://BookHip.com/SZXGKKQ

The Mystery Correspondent (Amazon)

Steamy Christmas novella, stand-alone – Ryder and Stella
Preview of The Mystery Correspondent: https://BookHip.com/X PBVAMB

Meet Him at the Altar (wide)

New Adult coming of age, written like a romcom/mystery
Kendall & The Groom
Preview of Meet Him at the Altar available on ELKoslo.com

Acknowledgments

F IRST, THANK YOU TO all my readers, whether this is your first book by me or you've been around since the beginning. Your support means the world to me and I wouldn't be on this journey without you.

Second, thank you to my alpha readers for this project. Katie, you continue to be my biggest cheerleader and thank you for encouraging me to channel a major disappointment into this book. Your friendship means the world to me and none of my books would be where they are without you. Kelly S., you've been with me for years, and I continue to be grateful for your enthusiasm, love, commentary on and occasionally much needed constructive criticism with my characters and storylines. Nikki, I love how you're always willing to drop everything and devour a rough draft. Thank you for always being in my corner. Amanda, while this was your first time as an alpha, you've been an amazing reader for awhile. Thank you for taking on this project and being there when I would drop random snippets and dirty character art into your DMs. Veronica, thank you for taking a peek at this one for me early and for your encouragement for the last few years I've been lucky to call you a friend.

As always, thank you to my amazing author friends, Danielle, Miguel, Lizzie, Ella and many others for always encouraging me to keep going, even when things behind the scenes threaten to knock me down.

And I couldn't do this without my husband who only teases me a little bit when I blush proofreading my own work. And for keeping me humble when I get a ghostface mask in the mail and only laughing at me for a few minutes straight.

.

Thank you to Brittni who got this one turned around quickly so we could get this dirty little novel into the world.

.

Make sure to follow me on Instagram - @ELKoslo_writes, Tiktok - @elkoslowrites and sign up for my newsletter at ELKoslo.com

.

Stay tuned next year for a steamy Valentine's Day Treat featuring our favorite grumpy bartender's little sister and his naughty best friend—Until next time,

.

E. L. Koslo

Social Media

Website: ELKoslo.com

Instagram: @elkoslo_writes
Threads: @elkoslo_writes
TikTok: @elkoslowrites & @elkosloauthor

Facebook: E.L. Koslo
Page: EL Koslo Romance Writer
Private Reader Group: E.L. Koslo's Dirty Words Brigade

Pinterest: @elkoslo

X: @ELKoslo
BlueSky: https://bsky.app/profile/elkoslowrites.bsky.social

Amazon: amazon.com/author/e.l.koslo

Linktree: linktr.ee.Elkoslo

Newsletter: https://elkoslo.beehiiv.com/

About E.L. Koslo

FIND THE FUNNY IN YOUR LIFE.

E.L. writes spicy romantic comedies with a variety of cinnamon roll heroes and strong heroines. She grew up in the midwest US, married her college sweetheart, now lives in one of those flyover states with her four spirited children and emotional support/writing companion Bernedoodle, Quinn. Banter and second-hand embarrassment are her jam, so be prepared to laugh with or at her characters.

Her novels combine her love of steamy romance, awkward but loveable leading males, and headstrong heroines with a dash of humor and a little bit of kink.